Gene

A First Romance

Cover photo obtained from Encore Editions
[old-orchard-me-from-end-of-pier]
Old Orchard, Maine, from the End of the Pier

From a different side of the country, but evocative nonetheless ...

Genesis of Love

A First Romance

by

J. R. Fisher

Rhymestone Arts
Sequim, WA

Dedicated to Ann and Pearl,
Dianne, Karen, Tracy and Megan

This is a work of fiction. Names, characters, corporations, institutions, organizations, places, events and locales are entirely the product of the author's imagination, or, if real, are used fictitiously. Any resemblance to actual persons, living or dead is entirely coincidental.

No part of this book may be reproduced, scanned, or distributed in any printed or electronic form without permission.

© J.R. Fisher
Rhymestone Arts
Sequim, WA
1999 and 2013

Chapters

Introduction. vi

Chapter One: Monday, August 1970. 9
Chapter Two: Tuesday. 47
Chapter Three: Wednesday. 76
Chapter Four: Thursday. 104
Chapter Five: Friday. 134
Chapter Six: Saturday. 170
Chapter Seven: Sunday. 227

Epilogue. 232

Introduction

This is my first novel, written in the summer of 1993. I had just graduated with a PhD in English literature from the University of Southern California and had every intention of spending the summer working up one or two more scholarly articles based on my dissertation on Book II of Edmund Spenser's *The Faerie Queene*. Instead, much to my surprise, I sat down and wrote *Genesis of Love*. As with most fiction, the book is loosely based on my own life experiences, including my getting sober in 1980. Tina is modeled on my first wife, Dianne, who died of breast cancer in 1984. But the novel is not set in the 1980s; instead, it is set in 1970 during the Vietnam Era. I was never in the military, but Tom is a veteran of that war. Again, as with most fiction, whatever facts began the creative process soon became fictionalized and absorbed into the larger story that became the novel.

This book was not published in the 1990s because my two daughters did not understand the novel as fiction. They saw it as their mother's story, thus biography. Any change in the facts as they knew them was understandably upsetting. So *Genesis of Love* was put aside for twenty years until all of us could heal. The sequel to this book was particularly upsetting to all of us, so I decided that neither book would ever be seen in print. But as they say, time heals all wounds.

My daughters are adults now, with lives of their own. Over the years, I've returned to the two books, continuing to edit them, cry over them, and prepare them for eventual publication. That day has now arrived.

My thanks to everyone who has read this manuscript over the years, including family and friends, most recently the Wednesday Writers of Sequim, Washington, who have seen the opening and closing chapters. Special thanks to Joseph and Barbora Cowles of Event Horizon Press, who published my first two novels, *The Adventures of J.R. Engels in the Great Pacific Northwest* and *Happy Valley USA*. They have become good friends in showing me the ropes of book design and publishing. Thanks to my wife, Ann, daughters Karen and Tracy, and granddaughter Megan, the women of my life. This book is especially dedicated to Megan, who never got the chance to know her grandmother Dianne. Hopefully this book will help fill the gap and explain the grandparents she does know.

For those of you who know me, the name J.R. Fisher is new. I've always published poetry under the name Jim Fisher, but when I was set to publish my first novel, *The Adventures of J.R. Engels*, I researched Amazon's listings for Jim Fisher and found that "he" had already published over a dozen books. The same was true for James Fisher and even James R. Fisher, to lesser degrees. We were forced to use James Randall Fisher, which is my legal name, but the only one who ever used it all at once was my mother. When I heard her say it, I knew I was in trouble. Fortunately, J.R. Fisher was available, and the J.R. nicely matches my narrator J.R. Engels in that first novel. Thus J.R. Fisher has been born.

JRF

Chapter One: Monday

August 1970

HE STOOD ON THE WOODEN PROMENADE, *looking out toward the water. Instead of postcard-bright California sunshine, the dawn was a half-hidden and restless motion behind unseasonable fog, a shifting and blanketing of the coast. Stretching and flexing to loosen his muscles, he started to breathe deeply. The scene before him was eerie, as fingers of grey mist crawled across the sand. With no actual sunrise to mark the difference, the light merely flowed into the dark, two sluggish streams merging to form a primordial soupiness. The morning had a poetic feel to it — a time made for thought and contemplation in a world without beginning or end, neither hot nor cold, light nor dark. In fact, it was a perfect morning for running because it was good for nothing else.*

Still in the loose sand, he began a slow jog until he reached the harder-packed, wet sand of the beach where he picked up the pace and shifted into a run, feeling the cool fog on his skin. He could see just far enough ahead to feel secure in this strange setting, but his only visual guide was the water line to the right.

Once he heard a sea gull but never saw it, like some brooding spirit over the waters, raucous yet haunting. Except for the gentle, muted splashing of the waves, the only other sound was his feet slapping down on the damp sand, creating a rhythm and a meter of their own in a timeless, foggy universe. On and on, he ran. Slowing once to get his bearings, he looked back, only to see his own footprints vanishing in the foam, as if he had never passed. No telling how far he'd run because there were no landmarks yet. Just he and the morning fog, thoughts and ideas racing through the elements.

"LOOK OUT!" Her voice, though distant and feminine, penetrated the lapping of the water and the murmur of the sunbathers, to reach into his consciousness, pulling him up from the pages of the journal, a yellow spiral notebook.

It came at him from behind and over his shoulder, out of a blind spot formed by the sun. Tom was already alert because of the warning. The shadow of the thing set his hands in motion, reaching for his gun. What gun? He had no weapon! This was crazy. Why would he have a gun on a public beach? Before he could fully react, the object whipped by his ear, a spinning, flapping whoosh of air. It was a towel, folded in half, the long way, and then tightly wrapped into a cylinder, the loose corners neatly tucked into the ends. The towel was maroon, a feminine shade with an extra touch of red. The cloth flapped a little as the cylinder spun. One tuck had worked loose, giving the missile a wobbly sort of flight.

His notebook went flying as the towel plunged down, hitting his right wrist. The missile drove on, striking him full and solid in the stomach. It would have knocked the breath out of him had it been heavier or had his muscles not been slightly flexed in anticipation. Part of him was caught in total surprise, while the other part was ready and had always been ready. The surprised part told him what had happened, registered the towel, colored like psychedelic blood, and started to calm the automatic responses.

This is California, not Vietnam, he told himself, even as the pulse continued to hammer in his head. *Slow it down, slow it down,* came the command, but that always alert, instinctive part of his psyche had already reacted. That part of him gave out a jungle yell, something more than surprise, much more. It was a primordial warrior shout of challenge, familiar and frightening.

Tom rolled in search of cover, reaching for the missing gun as he rose into a crouching position, one foot planted forward, with his back knee braced for the recoil. But of course there was no gun. He knew that, so he never fully raised his arms.

He was looking directly into her eyes — wide spread, soft brown, innocent, and totally surprised. For an instant, she was frozen in mid-stride, the expression on her face almost one of terror, but not quite, as if she did not have enough experience to be truly terrified.

The moment hung suspended, vibrating on its own isolated frequency, in its own space, a shiny ebony tube, just big enough to contain the two of them and nothing else. At the end of the tube, he saw the young woman centered in imaginary cross hairs. *My God,* he thought, *I could have blown her away!*

Tom saw her moving toward him again, but it was in slow motion and soundless. Then as she came closer, he heard her footsteps, even as he heard her voice.

"I'm so sorry," she said. "Are you all right?"

Slow it down, he told himself. *Breathe deeply.* Then she was kneeling at his side, her hands in motion, as if uncertain of what they should do. She was slim, probably college age, with short, dark hair, but she was not Asian, not Vietnamese. She was American, Caucasian and Californian. *This is the United States*, he reminded himself. *You are home.*

"Are you all right?" she asked again.

He just stared at her. Pretty and feminine, with a nice voice. Gentle, caring eyes, brown and deep, like river waters. She touched his arm then, a warm, soft, fluttering and bird-like touch. It was nice, very nice. It broke the spell.

"Yes, I'm fine — really." He even laughed. Automatic. In release. "God, I'm sorry I acted like that," he said. "It just surprised me." Slowing his breathing, he watched as she crawled two steps on her knees to reach his notebook. White sweatshirt over a black suit. Nice legs. Petite and tanned. "I hope I didn't frighten you?" he asked.

"No, it was all our fault. My friends were playing around with the towel, using it for a football," she said, her face puckering into a funny scowl, young but serious. "Here you are," she said, moving back toward him, holding the spiral notebook out for him to take.

Both of them were still kneeling, facing each other, as he took the notebook from her, continuing to stare into her eyes.

"My name's Tina," she said, smiling, a little nervously.

GOOD GRIEF, he thought, *who could blame her for being scared?* "Tom," he said, finally realizing how intently he must be staring. "I'm Tom. Glad to know you, Tina." He continued to study her, unable to stop looking. So long, in fact, that she smiled and glanced away, back to her friends.

"Come on, Tina," one of them said, but when Tom looked, all of the others — four, no, five people — were watching him from ten feet back where they stood in a semicircle. They were all on edge, anticipating something. What? Another outburst? Another roll in the sand?

"Well, I should go now," she said, rising to her feet. "Sorry, again." She laughed a little, nervously. After retrieving her towel, she moved off, looking back twice more. "Bye." She waved.

With pulse and breathing still slightly elevated, Tom stood up and returned to his own towel, where he sat down and leaned back into the canvas support. *Good God*, he thought, *I haven't had a flashback like that in months, so long ago now I thought they were over.* Tom glanced around at the sparse crowd, but no one else seemed to have noticed his reaction, just the girl and her friends. With luck, even they didn't realize what his actions meant. Mostly, he had maintained control. He had only rolled off the towel, not actually taken aim at her, thank God for that, not that a real gun even existed here on the beach. Everything considered, it had been all right, he supposed. As all right as something like that could be.

He watched the group as it moved away. In spite of what had just happened, his mind mechanically suppressed his emotions, recording the data. Her friends were typical California college-types — blond surfers, perhaps a football player or two, tanned girls in bikinis. A loose, friendly group that looked back at him guiltily, except for the big man who tried to put his arm around the girl's shoulders. She pushed it away. The man glanced back at Tom. His look was not from guilt but from challenge. Challenge of the species. Possessive. He must have thrown the towel because she seemed to be chewing him out. They were moving farther off now, so Tom could barely hear the words, but the man looked sheepish, then angry, by turns.

"He's nuts. You saw him." The man's voice. "He jumped like a bomb went off."

"You can't blame him for anything. It was you that did it." Her voice.

"The guy flipped out." The man again.

Flipped out. The words turned Tom's belly to ice because he had thought them himself, many times in the past. Wasn't it crazy to roll for cover, looking for a gun on a public beach? Probably so, but he'd been so well-trained in the military that the instincts refused to disappear. They would fade away for long periods, only to come roaring back when he least wanted them, usually under times of stress. Tom could no longer hear the girl's softer voice because of the distance, but the man's carried for a while longer.

"Get off my case, Tina."

Tom heard those words, clearly. What was he? A boyfriend? Idly, Tom continued to watch as the group moved down the beach, settling closer to the water. Three men and four women, now, as they were joined by another woman walking in from the other direction. A redhead. Every now and then, one of them would look in his direction, sometimes nervous, sometimes laughing. They were obviously telling the new woman what happened even while they teased the culprit who threw the towel. The man was not happy about the teasing and refused to look Tom's way again, by an effort of will it seemed. Twice the girl glanced at him and smiled, tentatively. *What was her name? Tina. Yes, that was it.* Eventually, her group settled down.

Leaning against the canvas backrest, Tom closed his eyes, forcing his body into the relaxation techniques he had learned in the VA hospital. They were necessary when he first came home from Vietnam, otherwise he couldn't sleep.

Now they were habitual. A purification. A ritual. Breathe slowly, gently. A modified meditation he could do at his desk when the pressure started to feel too familiar. In and out. Relax. Flow. Keeping the mind blank is very difficult.

When will they stop? he asked himself. *These damned flashbacks?* Without conscious awareness, he would find himself in a fire fight, usually being played out in fragments of sound and color. An explosion here. Red and yellow flashes of light. Someone falling there. Gun-fire. Whistles. Shouting. Sometimes the memories were so hypnotic that he forgot to come back, forgot they were just memories because they became more real than the world itself. Often it took a phone's ringing or a door's slamming to snap him back. Even with his eyes open, the memories had such power. Like now. His mind should be blank, in a meditative state, yet he still heard the sounds of the beach, the foot traffic, and the voices from the promenade. Even as he tried to empty his mind, the voices and sounds became another beach, in another world. He saw palm trees. Gunboats, all in a row. Invasion or withdrawal? Sometimes he could not tell. Victory? Defeat? It was all the same when you got too close. Close enough to smell the scent of death.

"Bang! Bang!" Snapping his eyes open, he saw a palm tree across the bay. Where? When? A sound. Again. There it was, on the road. Just a car coughing and backfiring on the highway. Just a car. Empty the mind? No use now.

She was watching him again, a look of concern on her face. Why? What had he done now? What had she seen? She shook her head to break free of his stare. Only then did Tom realize that he was still staring — blankly, darkly, completely. Staring into her soul and beyond. *You must not look at people like that*, he warned himself. *Plumbing their depths. Not here, not now, not back in the world. They get frightened.* He could see it in their reactions. While his thoughts ran on, Tom tried to stop looking at her. By sheer effort, he forced his eyes away. She did not deserve to be frightened. She was young, just a child really, a nice, innocent child who had tried to apologize for someone else's bungling. She had touched his arm. He could still feel it, tingling the hairs. Catching himself in time, he forced his eyes to another direction, down the beach, toward the ocean beyond the highway. Vacation paradise. But what kind of a vacation was he having? Relaxation? Restoration?

TINA WAS NO LONGER seething inside. Her anger at Ed was submerged, damped, hidden, defeated, dissipated. Thank God, he'd finally left to play volleyball with some of the other guys. Now, as she sat on the sand with her friends, Tina just felt neutral, empty, and strangely sad, almost as if she could cry. Only one week of summer remained before the start of her senior year in college. All she wanted today was a relaxing time at the beach, but then Ed showed up, the last person on earth she wanted to see. Now, look how everything had turned out, thanks to him. That prank with the towel was unforgivable.

"Here, let me carry your stuff," he said, when they met on the sidewalk, completely by accident, his small group joining hers. He moved directly to her side and took the rolled-up towel from her hand before she had time to react.

"Give it back, Ed. It's not heavy."

He started to return the package but then thought better of it, pulling the towel back, instead. "Come and get it," he teased, dancing away from her.

Why, she asked herself, *was he doing this?* How could he pull a stunt like this, after yesterday? "Ed, give me the towel, please," she said aloud. More than a little irritated, she watched as he lobbed the rolled-up bundle, like a football, to Troy, who tossed it back to Ed. Back and forth, getting more daring with each toss. *Maybe I'm wrong*, she thought. *He is an idiot.*

In her mind, Tina could still see the last toss of the towel as it arched over Troy's outstretched arms and then beyond the wooden railing of the promenade before it started to descend. She followed its flight, knowing exactly what would happen — the man holding the notebook would be hit by the towel. She knew it, she just knew it.

"Look out," she shouted, trying to warn him, but it was too late.

Remembering the scene still made her cringe. How would something like that feel, coming at you unawares, out of the blue? It would have scared her to death. How could anyone blame the man — his name was Tom — for acting the way he had? For rolling in the sand? Something like that could give a person a heart attack. Tina glanced over at the man, but he was concentrating on his book again.

She didn't know what to think. Crazy as it seemed, she could actually feel his intensity from across yards of sand, like emotional waves. Yet he didn't move, other than to look at her, once or twice. He had looked, so he was interested, but that didn't necessarily mean anything. After all, their lives had touched, if only for a moment. Such a silly thing, the towel. Surprisingly, she was interested too, but why? With everything else going on? This mysterious stranger, this Tom, was not her type—whatever that meant. Why had she even thought such a thing? What was "her type" anyway? Certainly not Ed, not any longer. She had been attracted to different types of men, physically and mentally, but never intensely so.

That was the key, the intensity — this man's intensity. Most of the guys she knew were day-to-day, have-some-fun, eat-a-pizza, and go-to-school types. This stranger was older. Too old for her. Still under thirty, probably, but somehow he seemed even older. Yes, it was the intensity. Why had he reacted that way to the towel, rolling on the sand? What had been going on in his mind when he closed his eyes for so long? Tina found herself drawn to him then, stronger than ever. Strange. Very strange. He was looking down the beach now, the other way, but she had the feeling it was to avoid her. Like the games people play with reflections in windows and mirrors. Look, but don't look. She shifted her position on the towel, turning her head toward her girlfriends. *Let it go*, she thought. *Forget about it.*

"It was okay, but I've seen better movies," Anna was saying.

"I'll go tonight with Larry," Maggie responded, "unless we just stay in, if you know what I mean." Sensual, shared laughter from both the women. "He flies back to school in a couple of days. Time to start shopping around, I guess."

"That's cold, Maggie," said Anna.

"Cold? I'm no nun, and I'm sure not gonna sit around all year waiting for him to come home. What about you, Tina?" Maggie asked, having noticed that she was watching. "Are you still dating Ed?"

"I guess so," she responded, unwilling to tell them of her decision, just yet.

"Well, don't sound so enthused about it."

"After that stunt with the towel, I'm anything but enthused."

"Oh, Tina, don't make such a big deal out of it," Anna joined in. "Ed's nice enough. He was just fooling around."

Maybe I am overreacting, Tina thought. *Who knows?* It wasn't just the towel, though. The towel was only a symptom. Two days ago, she and Ed had a silly little spat, over nothing really. Then yesterday, Ed had broken into her place, leaving a single red rose with a note that read, "I'm sorry. Love, Ed." Maggie would probably think that the whole thing was romantic. Big as he was, Ed had actually climbed through her kitchen window. I must have forgotten to close it when I went to mass, Tina reasoned, either that or he pried it open. In any case, he broke in. He broke into her home while she was at church. She couldn't help feeling the way she did. Violated.

Tina looked over to the courts, where the guys were off playing volleyball, Ed included. She had made it as clear as she could when he called later on to apologize once again.

"Ed, you broke into my house."

"Tina, I just crawled in the window and left the note and flower. It's not like I'm a criminal or anything."

"Ed —" she'd started to explain, again, but stopped herself. What was the use? He really didn't understand.

Somehow they had completely different value systems. The towel this morning was just a prank, an adolescent game. She did not like the game, but she could live with it. Her home was something else altogether, and yet he couldn't see the difference. Or was there a difference, really? The towel was a minor symptom of what the break-in represented. She was like a possession to Ed. He never considered that she might have interests, rights and values of her own, independent of his. Her role was to be on his arm, looking good, supporting his image. Only she knew how fragile that image really was.

Big Ed they called him. *What am I going to do, now?* she asked herself. *About him? About this mess?* Everyone just assumed they were a couple. How could they be, now? Maybe not even friends. It had always been a relationship of convenience, right from the start. Big and strong as he was, Tina didn't think he was dangerous, though he could be moody. Sure, he was a campus hero. A football player, but one who seemed to confine his violence to the field. Ed worshiped her — his words — telling her he loved her, over and over, until she hushed him up, unable to respond in kind. When he got too insistent, too physical, she broke up with him. He almost fell apart then, showing her a side of himself that no one knew, a weakness, a neediness.

"Please, Tina," he said. "I don't know what I'd do without you."

His pleading had touched her deeply, reminding her of similar and very old, childhood feelings. She actually felt sorry for him now, more than anything else. Ed tried to hide so much of himself behind the confident image — captain of the football team. When they got back together, it was on her terms and reluctantly so. That's the way he phrased it — your terms.

"I know you're Catholic, Tina. I won't push you until you're ready, honest. I just want to be with you."

He said all the right things. What could she do? Now, his breaking into her house changed everything. She refused to see him yesterday, telling him that it would be better if they forgot about dating for a while. Ed argued with her, at first, but finally agreed, sort of.

"We'll talk about it, Tina."

"There's nothing more to talk about, Ed," she said. "I don't like what you did. Not at all."

Would Maggie really think it was romantic? His leaving a single rose and a sweet note? Maybe so, but Tina was not about to ask her, even though she was lying not five feet away, with her eyes shut against the sun. Something about Maggie set Tina on guard. The simple truth was that she didn't trust Maggie, not completely, and had not since sometime in high school. Maggie would do anything to get her way, and she had proven it several times, especially when a man was involved. Still, I might have reacted too strongly about the towel, Tina admitted, but not about the house — that was different.

Tina lifted her head from the towel and propped it on her forearm as she looked at her friends. Bill had not gone with the other guys because he couldn't leave Lisa's side, not even for a moment. They were almost making out, right now, on the beach, in front of everyone. True love? True infatuation, that's for sure. But they were cute in a nauseating way. Oblivious to everyone else. Lisa's last name was Cooper, so ever since she and Bill started going together, they were called Bill and Coo. She was small and blonde, with blue eyes, and Bill was tall and gangly, with dark hair and a ready grin.

"Stop it, Bill," Lisa said, laughing as she pushed his hand away from her breast.

"My darling, my darling," he said, making kissing sounds as he crawled closer to her.

"Umm," Lisa purred, settling back against him, as one hand stroked her stomach, "that feels good."

Then they were quiet and private together, oblivious to the rest of the world, even on a public beach. It was difficult for Tina to watch them, but intriguing, too. When it began to feel as if she were spying, Tina looked away and put her head back on the towel, facing the other direction. She glanced at the stranger, but he was reading. Tina closed her eyes, lost in thought.

MONDAY, THE FIRST DAY of the work week, Tom reminded himself, putting the notebook to the side. If he were working, that is. It feels strange not to be going in. Not much of a vacation, for sure not a vacation. No sense of relaxation or release, just nerves and an emptiness. At least the weather has lifted. The warming air feels good. Very good. Stretching feels good, too. Maybe that's the secret — just feel, don't think? Time passes. Eyes closed. Just feel. Relax. But again noise intrudes, an irritant, like the buzzing of an insect. More and more people arriving all the time, getting louder every minute. Ignore them. Think peace and quiet. Quiet.

Eventually, he gave up and tried to read again, but even that could not hold his interest. He wondered how long he'd been staring at that same page, reading the same paragraph? No way to tell. He refused to wear a watch this week, this week of decision. Make it a Capital D in that one. The Decision. There would be no Time this week, for Time did not exist. Sighing, he looked back to the group and found her staring at him. It took the girl a moment to realize that he was looking at her, too. She smiled, nervously, and glanced away, like a child caught in the act. In a few seconds, she looked back, just checking, and smiled again, before turning toward one of her girlfriends.

Off and on, Tom watched the group, idly trying to determine its composition, its dynamics. Obviously, two of them were a couple. Flirting, teasing, kissing. But the others seemed unattached, casual, just friends at the beach. Three men and two women, originally. Gradually, the group grew larger, joined by others, then smaller as several drifted off, toward the volleyball courts. He saw a couple of university sweatshirts, so they all probably went to school here. The same school he might be attending. Graduate school. Doctoral program. Who was he fooling? Or was it whom? He'd better learn. How could he go back to school at his age? At twenty-eight?

Suddenly, he had an image of himself, sitting in a classroom. A door slammed behind him when someone entered, and Tom saw himself diving to the ground, pulling the pin on an imaginary hand grenade. Another flashback, like the one he'd just had here on the beach. How could he go back to school? Tom knew the question was nonsense, fear-driven, because he had just taken a class earlier that summer, the final class for his master's degree. He had made it through thirty units of night school without any such a reaction. He could make it through more. Fear was a powerful force, but not one he could let govern his life.

Two young women passed by his towel, talking as they went. Tom tried to guess their ages, but he had no ready frame of reference.

"He's so cute, I could just die," one of them was saying.

"I know, but what about his fraternity? Could you seriously go with a guy in Sigma Tau?"

"If he was as cute as Steve, I could."

"Are you going to buy that outfit we saw yesterday?"

"Maybe."

Good grief! These were just kids. University students, obviously, but what ages? Nineteen, twenty? Children in the bodies of women. Tom had done three years of military service after earning his bachelor's degree. Then three years in aerospace. Years and worlds apart. The whole idea was insane — his returning to college, full-time — and it had been from the start. Absolutely nuts. Again he caught the girl with the towel watching him. They both smiled and looked away together, as if by mutual agreement, but only after a slightly too-long, lingering glance. He turned back to the notebook, actually feeling himself blush. How long since he'd done that? A blush, no less! How long had it been? Just being in this town was making him act like a junior high school kid. Fourteen. Puberty. Next he would break out in pimples.

Feeling restless, Tom was unable to work, so he closed the book, stood up and started walking toward the water, thinking that a swim might do him some good. As he moved across the damp sand, he was reminded of the run he'd taken early that morning on this very beach. Now as he waded out and began to swim, Tom fell into that same familiar rhythm, the steady tempo of his running. Once again he was free, as his thoughts roamed at will, until almost before he knew it, his hand touched the side of the float, and he was jerked back into reality. The swim had relaxed him for the moment, just as the running always did, but it had been far too short. With a sigh, he pulled himself onto the raft and stretched out in the warming air.

UNDER HALF-CLOSED EYES, Tina studied the others, her friends. Maggie was a gorgeous red-head, auburn-haired really, with shimmering highlights. *Maggie was Maggie,* Tina thought, *leave it at that.* Two of the other girls she had known most of her life, having gone to the same schools with them, all the way into the local university. Lisa, short for Elisabeth, and Anna. Yes, they would remain friends while they were together. Would or could they stand separation? Probably not.

Tina's best friend, Grace, had left three years ago for an Ivy League school, Columbia, on a full scholarship. She deserved it, had worked hard for it. But I do miss her so, Tina thought. We write when we can and see each other during the summers, except for this summer because Grace was studying in Europe. She and I will be friends forever, Tina thought. We swore a sacred oath in the third grade when Grace's family moved into town. Distance affected the friendship but did not change it. Strange. Once they got back together, it was like they had never been apart. Hours and hours of talking. No one could replace Grace, and no one had come close, this entire summer. Tina missed her friend.

What about the men? The boys was more like it. None of them seemed serious about anything, least of all school. Most of them were more worried about getting drafted than graduating. All they talked about was the choice between going to Vietnam or going to Canada. Ed was serious about his football, of course, but that was just about it. Bill was on the verge of flunking out. If he and Lisa continued as they were, he would flunk. Always on academic probation, he never even picked a major until the counselor assigned to him forced the issue.

These were her friends. A week ago she would've said they were her good friends, her close friends, but, in today's mood, she saw them as acquaintances, nothing more. Long time acquaintances, to be sure, but not close, not intimate.

Nothing like the friendship she had with Grace. Tina stayed so busy all summer that the pain of separation from her best friend was pushed to the back of her mind. Now that she had some free time, she felt that pain deeply, so much so that she quickly tried to shake it off. *You're acting like a homesick kid at camp,* she told herself. *Grow up, Tina.*

Shifting back the other way, she looked in the stranger's direction, but he was gone! For just a brief moment, she felt a touch of panic, a feeling which surprised her. Yes, he was gone, but his backrest, towel, and book were still there. Where was he? She found the man, just as his feet hit the water. He waded out, then began to swim in the direction of the float, empty now that the afternoon was getting along. Before she realized it, she was on her feet.

"Anna, I'm going for a swim."

"Huh? Oh, sure. See you later," her friend responded, half asleep, now that they had settled into sunbathing.

Off I go, just like that! This is really crazy, Tina thought. Never. No, never in my life have I done anything like this. Blatantly follow a man? Never. But here I am, doing it. The water was cold on her feet. The shock of it almost stopped her resolve, but only for a second. Plowing ahead, she began to swim, drawn on almost against her will. *Why am I doing this? Stop thinking,* she told herself, *just swim, one arm in front of the other.* She had always been athletic, so her stroke was smooth if not powerful.

GRACEFUL, HE THOUGHT, as he watched her swim. *Contained, self-possessed. She's not shy in the water.* Now that she was getting closer, Tom grew certain about its being the same girl — Tina. Her towel on the beach was empty, but she could have gone off somewhere else. Soon she was close enough that he could recognize the shape of her head, the familiar way she moved, even in the water. She reached the float.

"Hi," he said, holding out his hand to help her up, onto the raft.

"You, too," she responded with a smile, gamin but genuine. She took his hand and climbed onto the float.

"Great day for a swim," he said, teasing her a little for following him out to the raft, but she just looked back, uncertain how to take the statement.

"Yes," she finally responded, non-committal, as she stood there, brushing the water off her arms and legs. After another second or two, she continued. "I wanted to apologize again for that towel thing."

"Forget it," he said. "It was nothing."

She swam all the way out here just to say that? he asked himself. Tom felt his own smile, wondering if she believed that herself. She sat down on the raft, and he watched as she squeezed the water from her hair and tried to comb it with her fingers. As they continued to make small talk, exchanging pleasantries, Tom grew more and more intrigued. It was always good for the ego to have an attractive woman come after you, but such directness, such brazenness, did not seem to fit this woman. In spite of his curiosity and cynicism, Tom relaxed and soon found himself enjoying the company.

"Are you a student at the university?" he asked.

"Yes," she responded, "Going into my senior year. I'll graduate next June, if they let me."

Tom felt himself smile, liking her sense of humor. "Did you do all four years here?" he asked her.

"Uh huh. I've pretty much done my whole life in The Shore — grade school and high school, too."

They continued to talk, basking in the summer warmth. On the float, they were undisturbed and isolated, as if alone together in the universe. Tom liked the feeling, even welcomed it, as he decided to leave his concerns back on the beach, at least for a little while. All time was now. No yesterdays, no tomorrows, just now. This moment.

"Are you on vacation?" she asked.

"More or less," he answered. "Actually, I'm thinking about moving here and going back to school."

"Really?" she asked.

Tom liked the way she seemed interested in his answer. He felt a spark and wondered if she did, too. "Yes," he said. "I've worked in aerospace for a while, but it's not what I really want — though the moonshot was great."

"You were part of that?" she asked, looking excited by the thought. "I stayed up all night watching it on television. Did you get to meet Neil Armstrong?"

"No," he said, feeling himself smile. "We had a very small piece of the action. My company worked on the guidance systems."

"I'll bet it was still exciting."

"It was," he admitted. "Our whole department was glued to a portable set someone brought in. Twenty people watching one nine-inch screen."

"Will there be another one?" she asked. "A lunar landing, I mean. I just read an article criticizing the space program because of the cost."

"There'll be others," he answered. "How many, I don't know." He shrugged his shoulders and closed his eyes, hoping she would drop the subject. The threat of layoffs was one factor in his decision about school. Tom was just as glad when she remained silent. He opened his eyes a few minutes later and saw that she had rested her head on her arms. Her eyes were closed. *Why did everything have to be so complicated?* he asked himself. *What would it be like to be young and innocent, again? Without problems?*

For a while, it was a beautiful day, full of light and California beauty, one to match her smile, but gradually, Tom became conscious of the sky's growing hazy, again, even as the temperature mounted. It was no longer overcast, but not quite clear, either. The temperature varied between warm but comfortable, and sultry hot, depending upon the breeze. Several times, when the air had completely stopped moving, the stillness became oppressive, not just hot, but heavy, as if a huge hand were slowly pressing the air down upon the sand and waters. Tom found conversation and even breathing itself difficult during these moments.

"Like an oven, isn't it?" he asked.

"Yes," she responded, growing silent, too.

Eventually, these times passed, as if the hand lifted and moved on, while leaving behind a certain echo, a memory of a previous passing and the expectation of one to come. Tom tried to remember when he had felt such a moment before. In Vietnam, he supposed. Lord knows, it was hot enough over there.

During one of the fiery emanations, the float became absolutely still as if all motion in the world had come to a stop. As the wave of searing heat passed over them, Tom watched a motor boat racing down the bay. The boat was beyond the marker pontoons, so it moved at an accelerated speed that did not fit anything he was experiencing, as if it were from another world altogether. The people on board waved and laughed as they sped by, creating a colorful, surrealistic contrast, like a Dali painting.

"Ahoy, on the float," one of them called.

"Hi," Tina hollered back, waving her hand in response. Tom merely nodded.

One minute they were here, the next they were gone. Even before their wake reached the float, the heat had begun to lift.

Tom looked at Tina, to see if the scene had affected her the same way.

"That was strange," she said, nodding in response to his look, letting him know the experience had been real. "This has got to be the hottest day on record."

"Do you really live here too, as well as go to school?" he asked. "I mean are you really from Golden Shore?"

"Yes," she said, smiling. "Born and raised. I've spent my whole life in this town. Is it so hard to believe?"

"No, it's really nice here. I can see why you'd like it, except for the heat. Up north we have hot days, too, but nothing like this."

"This is very unusual," Tina explained. "We only get a few days a year this bad. Santa Ana conditions, they call them, named for the Santa Ana winds, the Devil Winds."

Later, Tom heard Tina's name being called from the shore. Tina did not hear the voice until Tom pointed toward shore. They sat up together. Once conscious of the words, Tom realized the calling had been going on for a while.

"Tina, Tina." On the beach a woman was hollering her name and waving. When Tina waved back, the friend motioned for her to come in to shore, pantomiming by pointing to her watch, shouting something neither of them could understand.

"No," Tina responded, shaking both her head and hands. "I will stay here," she mouthed and pantomimed in return by pointing to the float.

Her friend did an elaborate shrug, using arms and hands as well as shoulders, then pointed back to the maroon towel, her sweatshirt and sandals. With both hands Tina waved her off, indicating it was okay. Leave the stuff. She would see her later.

WATCHING ANNA, Tina realized that most of the group had already left. The volleyball game must have ended, too, because the court was empty, the net gently swaying in the mild breeze. When had it ended? Who knew? Idly, she wondered where Ed had gone? Probably to get something to eat with his friends, that or off to afternoon practice. Funny, but it was the only time she had thought about him since swimming out to the float. Tina watched her friend walk back to the beach towels, pick up her own, and move off toward the promenade, joining with two of the others who were waiting for her.

When they settled back down on the float, Tom smiled and she smiled in response, feeling like a conspirator. Somehow, Tina felt like she'd just stepped through a doorway of sorts. She had chosen to stay on the float with a stranger, rather than be with her friends. Tina wondered what it meant. What had just happened? A psychic doorway on a float, like a passage into some new dimension? Something straight out of science fiction, maybe. Nothing had changed, really, yet everything felt different — nothing, everything. For that matter, what was she doing out here in the first place, with a stranger? But he was not really a stranger, not any longer. For a minute, they were quiet, and she felt awkward, but soon they were talking again, as if they had never been interrupted. It was already forgotten, she sensed.

"Where do you live up north?" she asked, realizing she had never asked earlier. If he mentioned it, she had forgotten.

"Monte Vista."

"Is it nice?" she asked, suddenly eager to learn all she could about this man, this stranger, this Tom.

"Yes. It's not a tropical paradise like this, but I like it. The mountains have their own kind of beauty."

PLEASANTLY SURPRISED, Tom realized that he was enjoying himself, just by being in her company. She'd chosen to stay with him, rather than go off with her friends. That said something, didn't it? But what? He decided just to go with the flow and actually started to relax, to enjoy the beach, as if this could be a real vacation after all.

"So, what's it like growing up by the ocean?" he asked her.

"Nothing but volleyball and weenie roasts," she laughed, "sunny days and warm water. Don't you ever get tired of all those squirrels in the mountains," she said, kidding him.

"They're not bad with mustard and catsup," he joked.

"That's terrible," she said, making a face, but laughing.

"What's the university like?" he asked, curious, and more than willing just to listen to her.

As Tina began to describe the school, Tom lay back and watched her. Tina was propped up on her elbows, so, at first, it took a little effort for him to focus on her eyes instead of her cleavage. Moving his head slightly, he forced his attention on to her face. Every now and then, she would ask him a question, but he moved the conversation back to her as soon as he could. Tom did not want to talk about himself, not today. It felt good to put his problems, his decisions, to the side for a while. He was tired of listening to his own head, his thoughts going round and round, in endless circles, like the proverbial squirrel cage. It was far more pleasant listening to Tina. She was a good conversationalist, entertaining, and fun to be with — and very attractive.

"It's still the smallest school in the system," she was saying, "which is one reason I like it."

"Have you taken any English classes?" he asked, forcing his eyes to meet hers instead of running over her body.

"Oh, the usual — freshman composition. Why do you ask?"

"Just curious. I've always liked English."

"Me, too. Funny, but it's supposed to be my minor. At least it was when I started, but I haven't had time to take any literature courses. Just those required for the teaching credential. Children's Literature."

As she talked, Tom let his mind drift to the coming semester. Would or could he really be here, in Golden Shore, taking some literature courses of his own? Right now, everything seemed possible in this dream world.

Time passed. How much, Tom had no idea. Looking past Tina's shoulder, he became aware that someone else was swimming out to the float. It was a man, big and not much of a swimmer at that. Instead of gliding through the water, cooperating with the medium, the man was fighting his way to the float by sheer brute force.

"What did you say?" Tom asked, realizing he had lost track of what Tina was relating.

"I was just telling you about my friend, Grace, who's studying in Europe. She goes to Columbia but is spending a summer at the Sorbonne. What's wrong?" she asked.

"We have company," Tom said, nodding back toward shore.

Tina turned just as the man took the last two or three clumsy strokes and grabbed for the side of the float. He pulled himself up onto his forearms, gasping for breath, with his body still in the water. The float rocked with his arrival.

"Ed? What are you doing here?" Tina asked, sitting up, obviously surprised by his sudden appearance.

For a few seconds, the man said nothing until he'd caught his breath. Tom noticed his powerful forearms and the well-developed neck muscles. This Ed was no swimmer, but he was in good shape. The man was soon breathing normally again, almost instantly. A quick recovery, an athlete's recovery, Tom gauged from his own experience as a runner.

"Come back with me, Tina," the man said, then paused for a quick breath. "I want to talk with you."

Tom noticed that his words held more of a demand than a request. *He must be her boyfriend,* Tom reasoned. *For sure, he was the same one who had thrown the towel.* The blond man looked from Tina to Tom, and Tom did not like what he saw in the man's expression, even though Ed tried to shield the expression by quickly looking back at Tina. The message had been clear. *Great,* Tom thought. *Here I am, right in the middle of a lovers' quarrel.*

Tina was so slow in responding that Tom looked away from the man and back toward her. Almost imperceptibly, Tina moved toward Tom and away from the big blond man in the water, only by an inch or so, but Tom noticed the movement and saw that the man had seen it, too. Ed's eyebrow twitched once, as if from a tic, when he looked down at her hand on the float's surface, the hand that had pushed her away from him. Tom took in all these details, filing them away for future reference, on an automatic record mode. He was poised, waiting for something to happen. Now what?

SHE FINALLY MANAGED to speak, "No, Ed. I'm going to stay here for a while." Her heart was pounding. Surprise? Fear? She didn't know which. Maybe both.

"You've been here all afternoon, Tina. I want you to come with me."

"Ed, this isn't the time. We've already talked. Remember?"

Tina couldn't read the look on Ed's face, but she knew it was one she had never seen before, in all the weeks they dated. She did not like the look and could feel herself cringing away from it. Now, Ed was looking at Tom, in much the same way, but with the emotion more unveiled. Hate, perhaps, or jealousy? Ed made an effort to hide the feelings by looking back at her. For a second she saw a look of hurt come into his eyes, then suddenly he moved, in a surge of power.

"Fuck it!" he shouted, pushing away from them, leaving behind a spray of water. The float rocked for a moment from the sheer force of his pushing off. Instinctively, Tina dodged the water that fell over her and Tom. Then she watched as Ed continued on toward the shore, using over-powered, angry strokes. Tina could feel herself shivering slightly as she followed his movements. *My God,* she asked herself, *do I even know him at all?*

"Are you all right?" Tom asked, after a long pause, during which the float stopped rocking and settled back to the gentler rhythm of the sea.

"I think so," she answered, quietly, but then had an irrational thought pass through her mind — *Where are my manners? I should have introduced them, Tom and Ed* — but the absurdity of the idea was instantly obvious. Now, wouldn't that have been good? Introduce them, indeed! Her mind whirled from one random thought to another as she stared at Ed's back while he plowed through the water.

"You're sure?" Tom said, but the words never really registered until he reached out a hand and touched her knee — just once, briefly.

"What? Oh, yes. I'm fine," she said, looking at her knee, where he had touched her.

"I hope that I haven't — you know," Tom was saying. "That I didn't mess you up, somehow?"

"Oh, no," Tina answered him, looking up to see a concerned expression on his face. "In fact, Ed and I just broke up. That's all. It has nothing to do with you. I thought he understood how I felt, but I guess not."

"You're really sure? He doesn't seem in too good of control right now," Tom responded, hesitantly.

"He'll be all right," Tina said, with more certainty than she felt.

By the time she looked back toward the shore, Ed had reached the boardwalk, climbed the stairs and was already turning the corner, walking up toward PCH — Pacific Coast Highway. As far as she knew, he never looked back. Once again, the image of a doorway came to Tina's mind, but this time the door had slammed shut, leaving her on the other side, the outside.

"I don't mean to pry —" Tom said, after another long pause, obviously waiting for her to say something first, if she were ready. "It's none of my business, but are you sure you'll be all right?"

Tina looked into his eyes and was pleased to see real concern, not just polite formality. Tom really was a nice guy. He deserved better than walking into the middle of this mess. Lord, it had all started with that towel's scaring him half to death. She smiled and he smiled back. Surprising herself, Tina felt she could trust this man. It was a nice feeling.

"It's been building up for a while, I guess," she started out, hesitantly at first, "but it all came to an end yesterday. We had a silly spat last week. Then yesterday morning, while I was at church, Ed broke into my house."

She paused for a minute, trying to gauge Tom's reaction, gauge it against her own reaction. Was it that big of a deal, really? The break-in?

"He doesn't have a key?" Tom asked.

"A key?" Tina responded, shocked at the question.

"I just assumed he was your boyfriend — you know."

"Oh, no!" she said, feeling herself blush when she realized what he had assumed. "We don't live together — nothing like that. No, he doesn't have a key. He must have forced a window open and crawled in that way."

"He really did break in, then? Did he damage the place?"

"No," she said, again, hesitating to tell him the whole story, but then she did so anyway. "Actually, he left a nice note, apologizing for the fight, and a single rose. Maybe I'm making too big a deal out of it?"

"Well," he said, "I guess that depends on how you feel about it."

"How would *you* feel?" she asked him, the question coming out of the blue, something she might have asked her friend, Grace, but certainly none of her other girlfriends, which came as a sudden realization because she had *not* asked any of them, and she'd had the chance to do so.

"That's what I was trying to figure out," he answered her, with a wry smile that he tried to disguise, but couldn't.

"What's so funny?" she asked, a little taken aback by the smile which had turned into a grin.

"I guess I haven't had too many women break into my place. I don't know how I'd feel about it."

Suddenly, she saw the humor, too. It was a little comical thinking about a man's getting upset over a woman's aggression. Maybe that was a sexist attitude, but it was funny, nonetheless. Tina felt herself starting to grin, and then they were both laughing. It felt good to laugh, a nice relief. Once again, Tina experienced that strange sensation of having passed through a doorway. She had no words for the experience, other than the sense that something had changed, leaving her with the comfortable but exciting knowledge that a new door was opening ahead of her, not just one closing behind her.

AS THEY SAT on the pier, later, Tina watched the light starting to give way to darkness. There would be no glorious color display, not tonight. Sometimes the evenings were better than fireworks, but today the sky had grown overcast, and the very air felt as if a heavy fog would roll in again.

"Too bad it's so murky," she said. "It can really be pretty out here."

"Maybe it'll clear up before the week's over," Tom said, almost as if he were asking her opinion, as if he hoped it would be so.

"It should," she answered, glancing at his profile as he looked across the pier railing toward the water. Tina was conscious of how comfortable she was with Tom. It felt very good. Warmth against the fog.

They had stayed on the float after Ed left, until the wind picked up, driving the temperature down. Swimming back together, in no hurry, they retrieved their towels and gear, cleaned up a little at the showers, then moved off toward the pier, without making any real plans. Dinner was casual, just hamburgers and french fries, with cokes to drink, at Lucy's Cafe, a favorite place of hers, warm and friendly. Lucy, the owner, knew all the locals and had smiled seeing Tina with Tom. Afterwards they walked out to the end of the pier and sat on one of the concrete benches, in spite of the changing weather. They continued to talk, their sweatshirts being enough protection against the evening air. Eventually the air turned so heavy that they could see only because of the eerie, chalky glow from artificial lights placed high on concrete poles, spaced every twenty yards along the pier.

Later, during a pause in their conversation, Tina tried to remember what they had just talked about — anything, everything, nothing — it didn't seem to matter. She realized that she'd done most of the talking.

"I'm sorry for jabbering on so much, Tom. I'm not like this usually."

"Don't be silly," he said. "I enjoyed it."

It was unusual for her to talk so much, but he was a good listener, and she really needed to talk — she had unloaded a summer's worth of conversation. All the things she would have told Grace, had she been here. Funny, but what had she really learned about Tom, other than she liked him and he was a pleasant companion? As the evening wore on, she felt herself becoming shy. What next? Tina grew nervous when he asked if they were close to her place, or if she had driven to the beach.

"No, I live just a couple blocks from here."

"I'll walk you," he said.

These were the high-tension moments she always hated, why she usually preferred dating in groups. Would he ask to come in? What would she do then? Tina was surprised and relieved when they reached her house because he did not ask. Instead, they talked for a minute longer on the sidewalk, leaning against the retaining wall, the fog surrounding them like a cocoon.

"Nice place," he remarked, glancing at her house, then around at the neighborhood, as much as could be seen of either through the grey mist. "At least I think so," he added, with a smile.

"Thanks. I like it," she said. "Everything's old and quaint, and small here in The Shore, but it's home."

"You could do a lot worse."

"I was really lucky to get a place this close to the water. In the daylight, you can see the beach and the ocean — long distance, but not bad."

"Sounds nice," Tom said, idly, as both of them seemed to realize the day was over at the same time.

He did not even try to kiss her. Instead, Tom thanked her for a pleasant afternoon and absently reached out to touch her hair.

"Will you be on the beach tomorrow?" he asked.

Surprised by the touch, which still continued, she just nodded yes.

"See you then," he responded and was gone into the mist.

Tina could still feel the gentleness of his touch on her temple. What had it been? She reached up and touched the spot. A curl out of place? She had barely rinsed out her hair on the beach. It had to look a mess. What did the touch mean? A caress? Affection? It was nothing staged, nothing like a move he was putting on her. She had a feeling that, if asked, he would not even remember doing it. A gesture, an instinct. It felt right, even a little exciting, but mostly it was a reassurance, an acknowledgment, a thank you.

The more she thought about it, the less certain she grew. Had it really happened? Yes. Surely. But the memory of the touch grew confused. Why hadn't he kissed her instead? What would she have done had he tried? As she walked up to the porch, she could still feel the afterglow of the touch, like an electricity on her skin and hair. Yet now it seemed more like a gesture that a big brother might make toward a little sister. A gesture of affection. Brotherly and fraternal. Nothing more. She was strangely disappointed. It had seemed so right a minute ago. Now it seemed too little. Not nearly enough.

HOURS LATER, Tina lay in the tub, going over the day, but deliberately trying not to think about Ed and their breakup. It was hard to shake the image of his pushing away from the float. She'd never seen him that angry — almost furious. Every time the picture surfaced, she pushed it back under her consciousness. She also tried not to think about Tom, simply because she didn't know what to make of the whole thing and was afraid to hope for too much. She didn't even know how long he would be in town. He'd been a little vague about his plans, saying something about an appointment at the university, but he hadn't explained in any detail. The suggestion was that he might start graduate work, but he wasn't really sure, yet.

While the bath water was running, Tina had shampooed her hair in the bathroom sink. Thank God she'd cut it extra short for the summer. At first, the bath had been just right — so hot she could hardly stand it. Water to soak in, to relax in, to think in. Now, it had grown tepid, even cold, as she reached out a foot to turn the hot back on, twisting the knob with her toes and the ball of her foot. All the bubbles were long gone, now. She loved a bubble bath, and had ever since she could remember. As the water ran, she looked at herself, critically. Why did such appraisals make her feel so guilty? Something to do with the Church? Original sin, perhaps? Feminine vanity? She had a nice figure. Her girlfriends told her they were envious, and she caught her share of looks from men on the street and especially at the beach. But those looks always made her nervous and sensitive, so she opted for the more conservative suits. A bikini, yes, but nothing like the ones some of her friends wore. Lisa, for instance, whose bikini bra was a push up — it was under-wired and barely there, really, just a single piece of fabric that showed her nipples when the suit was wet. Showed them even when dry, for that matter. Especially after she and Bill had been fooling around, they stood out. Looking down at her own breasts, Tina was surprised to see that her nipples were erect. Feeling guilty, angry, she sat up quickly, turning the hot water off, so quickly that some of it spilled over the side of the tub.

"Damn," she thought aloud, mopping it up with a towel.

Settling back into the steaming water, she still felt irritated beyond the immediate cause.

"Damn, damn, damn."

TOM PICKED UP his current journal and reread the piece he'd begun that morning. He had described the run on the beach in third person to achieve some literary distance. It worked. He liked the piece, but he had no place to go with it:

> On and on, he ran. Slowing once to get his bearings, he looked back, only to see his own footprints vanishing in the foam, as if he had never passed. No telling how far he'd run because there were no landmarks yet. Just he and the morning fog, thoughts and ideas racing through the elements.

Tom turned the page and filled several more in a rush. Surprisingly, or maybe not, really, most of these pages had something to do with Tina. It had been a pleasant day, and she was a nice person, after all. A nice distraction.

He wrote some dialogue, but mostly it was images and descriptions. The warm brown color of her eyes and her dark hair. The healthy look of her tanned skin. The careful way she phrased her words, especially when she was teasing or going for a mild joke. Her smile. After thinking about it, Tom still didn't know why she'd followed him to the float — escaping from the boyfriend, maybe — but he was glad she'd done it. She hadn't been trying to pick him up, nothing that obvious. No, that just didn't fit with her personality. She was a curious blend of innocence and independence. Still, pleasant as she might be, Tom asked himself what future there could be for the two of them? Silently and on paper, he asked it.

"Strangers passing in the night? Just accept the good things," he wrote, then added, finally, "Don't analyze everything to death." Who knows? Tomorrow she might make up with the big guy — Ed was his name — though Tom doubted that would happen from her reaction on the float. For her sake, he hoped it wouldn't happen. Ed was the one who'd accused Tom of flipping out. Now Tom wondered if the reverse might not be true?

When he turned the page and tried to work on fiction, Tom came to a wall. As a runner, he was familiar with the same term, used in a different way, perhaps, but analogous. Or was it? The wall for a runner could be overcome, broken through. But this writer's wall — this writer's block — that he kept encountering seemed impenetrable. Try as he might, he could find no doorway through it. He could not get beyond a word or two at a time. Journals he could manage, with a struggle, but nothing more serious. It was the same thing tonight. He could write about Tina, but when he attempted to write about an incident in Vietnam, the words would not flow. Flow? That was a rich one! He couldn't drag them out, no matter how hard he tried.

Tom walked out onto the landing in front of his second-floor rental apartment, feeling distracted, disjointed, separate. He had wanted a view, but this was the best his travel agent could find — a mere glimpse of the ocean between two other buildings, and not even that much now, with the fog rolling in — just a sliver of a view that had cost him a fortune for the week. Surprisingly, he thought of having a cigarette. In high school and college, he had never smoked much because of his interest and participation in sports, but he had picked up the habit in the military. He quit smoking once he was back home and running regularly again, but occasionally he still felt the urge — like now — when his frustration level reached this point. He also thought about having a drink, one of those random ideas that still came every now and then, without his volition. Tom just smiled and sighed, letting the idea fade away. *That's the last thing I need — a drink. As if one had ever been enough.*

All things considered, the day had been good. The night was beautiful and mysterious, dark and quiet. Why couldn't he just sit down and write?

QUESTIONS SWIRLED through Tina's mind. *How many times had she refilled the water? Was she going to lie here forever? What would happen tomorrow? With Ed? With Tom?* Over and over, almost against her will, Tina thought about that parting touch to her hair, to her temple. The sensation was gone now, the electricity having faded away, washed off with the shampoo and the steaming water, and with the perspiration that trickled down her cheek.

"Virgin," she thought aloud, against her will, hating the word even as her mouth gave it form.

The Church has done a real number on me, Tina thought. Holy Mary as a model, all the way through Catholic elementary school, as they wore those silly tartan plaid skirts. Hating the uniforms, yet liking the uniformity, how could she have made it through the Sixties intact? The Love Generation? One by one, her girlfriends had lost their virginity. Lost it? What a joke. Gave it up, sold it, gleefully spread it around, like jam and honey, had it stolen from them in back seats at drive-ins — but not one of them had really "lost" it, like some misplaced sock. Yet here she lay, twenty-one years old and a full-grown adult, sweating in a too hot bathtub, having just been patted on the head like some little kid, and a virgin still.

A loyal Catholic girl, a true believer. She reached up a hand and felt the place on her temple where Tom had touched her, letting herself envision his face. All things considered, the day had been so good. How could she end it by feeling so upset?

"Damn, damn, damn."

Chapter Two: Tuesday

"IN THE BEGINNING," Tom read from the real estate brochure he was using as a bookmark, "God created a New Eden in the West." He supposed that the Swedish-looking blond on the front cover was meant to be Eve, in spite of the yellow bikini and the pose, as she draped herself languidly backwards against a palm tree, with one leg bent at the knee in a provocative angle. Other than the text itself, the biggest clue to the symbolism was the large red apple in the model's hand, which she held out toward the reader, with a tempting, pouting smile.

"Some Garden of Eden," he said aloud, looking up from the pamphlet. At least the fog had finally lifted, even if the sky remained a little overcast, and the beach was still pretty much deserted though the air was already beginning to warm up. Tom looked down again at the pamphlet, and, after shaking his head over their use of the Eden myth, he continued to read the glowing words of their Chamber of Commerce.

"Come to Golden Shore and enjoy the Sun, Sand and Surf of Southern California."

All the S's looked and sounded like snakes, though he doubted if that part of the biblical allusion was intentional. After that, the imagery fell flat as discussions of business opportunities and improved housing filled up the rest of the brochure. Closing the pamphlet, Tom caught himself looking at the cover again because the scene reminded him of Vietnam, not the model, but the blinding sun, the palm trees, and the beach. In the distance, he could almost see fire and smoke, and the incoming choppers.

The stress of combat was not the gunfire and the flames — they were bad, of course — but far worse was the ongoing, never ending, grating pitch of nerve endings, poised to spur the body into action. Stress, tension, and insomnia — he hated the feeling they invoked, like he was some over-wound mainspring in a clock. *Try for peace and quiet*, he reminded himself. *Let the jungle go.*

Slowly returning to the present moment, he heard something muffled. It was laughter, coming from behind him on the boardwalk, where the noise level continued to rise as more and more people came to the beach. Boisterous and young. Ignore them, he told himself, leaning into the canvas backrest, as he tried to force his interest onto the book he still held. Think peace and quiet, peace and quiet. Yes, let the jungle go.

WHEN TINA GOT TO the beach, he was already there, in the same place as yesterday. The scene jolted her for just a second because it seemed to be exactly the same, as if his beach chair had never moved — like some kind of a science fiction time warp. She stopped on the promenade, looking down and across the sand at his back. Now she could relax. She had been hoping he would be here, but doubting it, too. Still, she did not move, not yet. A reluctance? A nervousness? Instead of going down the steps, she looked at the panorama stretched out before her, having been too caught up in her own thoughts to really see it before. What a glorious day! The sky was powder-perfect blue and cloudless, almost perfect enough to be a prayer. From this angle she could see where the sky met the sea across the highway, forming a horizon that went on forever and ever, without end. Amen.

"Hello," Tom called. He had turned around and was watching her.

"Hi," she responded, waving. Still feeling strangely and vaguely reluctant, she walked to the steps and went down to join him on the sand.

"So, how are you this fine morning?" he asked, shading his eyes against the sun as he looked up at her.

"Very well, kind sir," she responded, spreading her towel next to his.

A minute or two later, she tried to recall that early feeling of reluctance. Why had she hesitated? Once they started talking again, everything was fine. But for just that first moment, she had wanted to turn and run. Well, maybe not run, but walk away. *How silly*, she thought.

When Tom asked her more questions about the university, she wondered if he were just making conversation or if there were something more to his curiosity, like a real possibility of his attending the school.

"Well," she began, "it's mostly a commuter college — but that sounds funny for a university, doesn't it? Commuter university — is that any better? It's the smallest school in the state system, except for a brand new one out in the valley. Not too many people live on campus, so the social life is pretty much up to you."

"Any demonstrations?"

She knew exactly what he meant. After all, the Kent State shootings were just a few months ago, an event still on everyone's mind.

"Not much, really. There was a sit-down strike in one of the administration buildings last semester, but it never amounted to anything."

"I wondered if there would be picket lines and the like."

"Not yet," she answered, "though the news is always full of stuff about the peace movement."

"Yes, I know."

Something about the way he said that made her look from the water to his eyes, but he had already turned slightly in the other direction, so she couldn't read much in his expression.

"Were you in the service?" she asked.

"Yes, for three years."

Tina sensed from the quiet but final way he'd said the words that he didn't want to talk about it, so she didn't press him. She thought she could guess at his feelings because her cousin, Frank, had just been discharged the year before. He had volunteered, thinking it was the right thing to do, but in the short time he'd served, the national climate had shifted even further toward the growing peace movement.

"My cousin, Frank, just got out last year," she said, trying to keep it as neutral as possible. "He was stationed in Germany,"

Tom did not respond, other than nodding once. Instead, he continued staring out to sea.

For sure he doesn't want to talk about it, she thought. Tina wondered if he could have been in Vietnam? The thought chilled her as she remembered his reaction on the beach yesterday, when he had rolled in the sand. She felt a sudden wave of sympathy for Tom. When Frank came home, still in uniform, a couple of kids on the street had booed him and one even spat at him. Maybe something similar had happened to Tom?

They were quiet for a while, until Tina tried to turn the conversation back to his questions about the university.

"Are you really thinking about going back to school?" she asked.

"Silly idea?" he asked, looking at her. "Going back at my age?"

"Oh no, not at all. A lot of my Education classes are scheduled at night because of teachers coming back for a credential or a master's degree. The evening classes are always more interesting because of the older students. They have a lot more to offer, in experience, I mean."

"We'll see," he said.

The day passed. Two or three of her friends stopped by to say hello, actually nosing around for an introduction, especially the auburn-haired Maggie.

"Tom, this is Maggie. Maggie, Tom."

"Hi, Tom, how are you?"

"Good, thanks."

"You look like an athlete," Maggie remarked, while giving his body a frank appraisal. Tina saw the look and felt a surge of emotion within herself. In that instant, she hated Maggie, and hated herself for feeling that way.

"I do a little running," Tom responded.

"Do you ever get caught?" Maggie asked him back, tossing the hair off her brow with a flick of her head, the message clear. At least it was clear to Tina. Maggie was shopping around already, and Larry had not even left town yet.

"Sometimes," Tom said, smiling.

Tina caught herself feeling utterly, foolishly jealous; but, no matter how juvenile she thought the emotion, she couldn't suppress it. How could Maggie be that brazen? She might just as well put a sign on her forehead — Available. Ready and Available. Come and get me. Maggie stood there in a practiced pose Tina had seen before — one hip cocked, legs together, but with one slightly bent at the knee, and both legs flexed to show their length, while her shoulders were pushed back to emphasize her breasts. No, Tina was not about to ask Maggie to join them, but Maggie was painfully slow to get the idea.

"Guess I'll be moving along, then," she said, reluctantly, giving Tina a veiled look. "See you around, Tom. Bye, Tina."

"She seems nice," Tom remarked, watching Maggie as she walked away.

"Uh huh," Tina responded, as neutral as she could make it, looking from Tom's face to Maggie's swaying backside. Now Tina understood why some of her friends avoided Maggie like the plague, her women friends, anyway.

As time passed, several more of Tina's acquaintances stopped by, but after meeting Tom, they didn't seem to know what to do. They just made small talk and then drifted off down the beach to where a larger group was forming. When Tina did not invite them to sit and made no move to join them, her friends just went about business as usual.

"Good grief," Tom remarked, after the third or fourth introduction, "do you know everyone in town?"

"I have lived here all my life," she answered, "but most of these people I know from school."

Once, later on, she saw Ed by the volleyball courts. Some sixth-sense told her that he had been watching her, but that she had just missed his prying eyes. His body motions said that he would not look this way, again, denied that he ever had looked this way. When she checked later, he was gone.

Tom told her he had some sort of a meeting that night, so they decided just to spend the day at the beach, doing nothing special, other than relaxing. Tina sensed that they had run out of small talk and were not quite ready to move on to serious subjects, content for a while to stay on this plane of getting to know each other. It felt like the first day of camp, when you chatter with someone, trying to see if you could be friends. Eager and interested, but holding back a little, too. Nothing serious, just talking and more talking.

At first, refusing to join the regular gang had made Tina feel adventuresome, even rebellious, especially by not joining up with Maggie or asking her to join them. Now, Tina realized that she was effectively isolated, separated from her friends, by choosing to be here with Tom. She wasn't completely sure that she liked the situation. As time passed, there were long periods of silence between them, as they each read paperback books. Tina noticed that Tom had a different book from yesterday. Had he finished the other one, already?

"Do you read a lot?" she asked, trying to make conversation in order to break her fretful mood.

"Compulsively. You?"

"Not as much as I'd like. Mostly textbooks these days."

"I know how that goes," he added, sympathetically. "Do you like fiction?" he asked, after a pause.

"Yes."

"What kind?"

He asked in such a way as to seem more interested in her answer than she'd normally have expected, as if it were not an idle question. She tried to answer as best she could, naming the last couple of books that she could recall reading, both of them juvenile novels that had been recommended in a Children's Literature course, but when she finished, he just nodded, without any further explanation of his interest.

Occasionally, she glanced at him, more often after she realized how deeply he was concentrating on his own reading. Her current book was a romance that one of her friends had given her. It was so ridiculous, silly actually, that she found herself on the same page for a long while, spending more time watching Tom than reading. She enjoyed the silence, happy that he did not feel some adolescent obligation to impress her. But he could pay her a little more attention, she thought. Still and all, it was a pleasant day.

TOM WAS GREATLY ATTRACTED to her. Tina was her name, but he still thought of her as the girl from the beach. Sometimes he felt old beyond his years, certainly far older than the physical difference in their ages. She was a senior in college, so he probably had no more than six or seven years on her. But what a world of difference in those years! He had been places and seen things he wished he could forget. Was that part of the attraction? Her innocence? Her youth? When she looked down the beach, in the other direction, he studied her, carefully. Tom still had no explanation for why she had followed him out to the float yesterday. She was not easy and had not been trying to pick him up, yet here they sat. Interesting, to say the least.

There was a certain maturity about her, too, an independence that complemented her seeming innocence. It was an intriguing combination in a woman, especially one who was as genuinely nice as Tina. He couldn't remember her bad-mouthing any of the friends she had introduced. She didn't tear down anything, really. Not politicians, teachers, or her parents. Part of her physical beauty was her coloring. In California, the blond look was in. Even natural brunettes became blonds out here. Tina was a natural, brown-eyed brunette. Her hair was almost dark enough to be black. She tanned well, a color that fit with her hair and eyes. She was genuine. Tom liked that.

"Getting hungry?" she asked, smiling at him.

"What?" he responded, totally surprised to be caught staring.

He was also shocked by what she'd asked, his mind taking it sexually. His reaction must have been dramatic, almost flustered, because she looked confused in turn. Tom could almost see her mind working as she thought back on what she had just said, finally realizing why he was reacting this way. She blushed beautifully, from her neck all the way to her hair-line. Even her chest was flushed, down to the top of her bikini. Maybe beyond.

"I didn't mean it that way. You know." She started laughing.

It was infectious. He laughed, too. Good Lord, he even felt himself blushing again. Like a couple of kids, they laughed and laughed until it hurt his sides. When they could finally stop, they walked up to the pier and had lunch, giggling again when the food was delivered.

IN SPITE OF ALL their laughing together, being with Tom felt like she were dating her uncle. He was very polite and thoughtful of her in ways that many of the male friends her age were not. He opened doors, carried her things, asked what she wanted to do — all of the old-fashioned stuff some of the younger men had never learned. At other times, he was so distracted that he almost ignored her presence, as if she were ten years old and a pest. Curious! He'd never tried to hold her hand, even, or kiss her. When they got back to the beach, they settled down to reading and listening to the transistor radio she had brought. She couldn't tell what kind of music he liked because he seemed satisfied listening to anything she chose. Maybe they had similar tastes? Or perhaps he was content to let her have her way in everything? That thought actually irritated her. It would be like an adult taking a child to the zoo, letting the child pick the whole itinerary. She did not like the idea of being thought a child.

Perhaps he was gay? She had two male friends who were a homosexual couple, Michael and Gabe, but she had not considered that possibility's applying to Tom. Good grief, did she actually attract gay men? What in the world would that mean about her? Tina was polite and decent to the two gay men she knew, and always assumed they liked her because she didn't dislike them. Why should she? Who in the world were they hurting? She couldn't help wondering about Tom, now that she had considered the possibility. After all, he hadn't put one move on her in two days, that brief touch to her temple notwithstanding. After a few minutes of thinking like this, Tina realized that she didn't want Tom to be gay. She definitely hoped he was straight. In fact, she very much hoped he was straight!

Tina had her answer within a few minutes of thinking the question. One of the university cheerleaders walked by, a girl Tina knew on sight, but not by name, not without its being blazoned across her chest. Tom couldn't seem to take his eyes off that chest. She was a knockout, if you liked the type. A peroxide blond. Light hair. Dark eye-brows. Athletic body, tanned to a golden brown, a little on the muscular side from the cheerleading, with dancer's legs and a bust that looked like it had been inflated with a bicycle pump. Breasts that size belonged on a woman two-and-a-half feet taller than she. On top of it all, she wore a white lace, fishnet bikini that definitely had more holes than it had material.

She walks like a burlesque queen, chugga-boom, chugga-boom, and another thing — Tina caught herself thinking and stopped. She did not like having such negative thoughts about others, usually suppressing them or keeping them to herself, but now they embarrassed her, simply because of their vehemence. Why was she so upset with the cheerleader? Tom was still following her down the beach with his eyes, that's why. In fact, he was almost drooling.

She had gotten the answer she hoped for. Tom was not gay. But now she was sorry she had posed the question. Why didn't he look at her that way? She was no blond bombshell, but she was a woman, and sitting right next to him. Did he even know she was here? Apparently not. Now he was staring off across the bay, lost in fantasies about cheerleaders, no doubt.

THE BLOND REMINDED HIM of a nurse in the VA hospital. Just as good-looking and sexy. Probably just as much of a tease as well. Everybody on the floor tried to put the make on her. Lied about her. Made up stories about her. Even claimed to have scored with her. But she deserved every lie and every story. God only knows what perverse pleasure she took in torturing sick men. She brushed herself against them, hips, rear, thighs, making it seem accidental.

From behind, she could slide her breasts across your shoulders in such a way that a blind man could have sketched her naked. From the side, she rubbed herself on your biceps and forearms. She had the coldest, most sadistic eyes he had ever seen on a woman. Tom hated her.

Nurse Bambi had been good for him, however, ironically and abysmally good. All the men called her that. Her badge read only Lt. B. Smith, RN, so, with no known first name, Bambi she became. She was the first person Tom reacted to in the hospital. To his knowledge, no one ever asked her name. Tom doubted she would have given it. Or if she did that it would be her real name. Bambi took utter and absolute delight in torturing men. The more helpless and pitiful they were, the better she seemed to like it. Paraplegics, quadriplegics, psychotics, neurotics, catatonics. It made no difference to her.

When Tom was first brought into the unit, he was so withdrawn and shut down that Bambi ignored him for a while. But not for long. Within a week, as Tom sat staring out the window, she came up behind him and rubbed herself across his shoulders. In a quiet but clearly audible voice, intended only for Bambi, Tom told the woman that he would tear her head off if she ever touched him like that again. Ironically, it was a breakthrough. One of the male interns must have overheard the confrontation and reported it to his psychiatrist.

"Welcome back to the world, Tom," Dr. Sallivant had said.

"Get fucked," Tom told him, and from there they started to make some progress.

Tom often thought about the months he had spent in the VA. Mostly he remembered the doctor with fondness.

Richard was his first name, but his patients all called him Dr. Dick. Just the sight of the blond on the beach had the power to evoke all those memories. Anger and resentment. Number one on the list. Thank God something had broken through the shell, or he might still be there, locked up in the hospital, maybe in a padded cell. *Do I ever need a meeting*, he told himself. Sighing, he turned to his side and found Tina staring at him with a look that might make Bambi proud.

"What's wrong?" he asked.

"Nothing, nothing at all," she replied coldly, quickly looking away.

Now what was that all about? Tom wondered. It took the rest of the afternoon, but they parted on good terms. Trying to figure out what he had done wrong, Tom was solicitous of Tina, paid attention to her and got her to talk about herself. At first, she seemed suspicious of his attention and intention, but eventually they settled into the easygoing talk of the past couple of days.

Tom had to leave early in order to get dressed for his meeting, so they decided to have dinner separately. As he walked back to his apartment, Tom wondered if he were monopolizing too much of her time. Was that the problem? No, he didn't think so. She seemed to like his company, except for those few minutes this afternoon. He would see her tomorrow and play it by ear. Tom really enjoyed being around Tina, but if it wasn't mutual? He would just have to wait and see.

SHORTLY AFTER Tina got home, the phone rang. Surprisingly, it was Maggie calling to invite her out to dinner that evening — a first time for that — probably hoping that she would bring Tom; but since Sue was going, too, and Tina did not feel like sitting home alone, she said yes. Actually, she was a little irritated at Tom's reticence. Tina didn't really know what he was doing, just some important meeting. She had only known him for two days, but already he was irritating her, and more than a little. Not a good sign.

A minute later, the phone rang again, so soon after the first call that Tina assumed it was just Maggie calling back with more information. But it wasn't.

"Hi, Tina."

"Ed?"

"Yeah, it's me. How about a movie tonight, maybe some dinner first?"

"No, Ed. I don't think so," she said, trying to make it sound firm and final. Great, she thought, now what? Obviously, they still hadn't settled anything. Nothing final. Not from Ed's perspective.

"Why? Are you busy?"

She didn't like the way he said *busy*, almost snidely, somehow. "Yes, I've already made plans for the night."

"With him?"

Tina definitely didn't like the way Ed said *him*. Nor did she want to tell Ed what she was actually going to do for fear he would show up there. "No, Ed. I'm not seeing Tom tonight."

"Sure," he responded in that same tone.

"Ed, do you remember our last talk?"

"Yes."

"Well, none of this stuff between you and me has anything to do with Tom, none at all."

"I'll bet. See you around."

He hung up after that, without so much as a goodby, leaving Tina to stare at the receiver in her hand.

ON HIS WAY OUT, Tom stopped by his landlady's office.

"Welcome to Golden Shore," said the woman behind the desk, not recognizing him because the night person had actually given him the key. His landlady was a short, plump woman who had salt-and-pepper grey hair and wore a brightly-colored, flowered muumuu. "Just call me Gloria. Is this your first visit?"

"Yes, it is, but I'm already registered, up in Room 204," he reminded her.

"Oh, sure," she answered. "You came in late on Sunday. What can I do for you?"

"Would there be any problem if I wanted to stay through the weekend?"

"Let me check. It'll only take a second," she said as she pulled out her registration book. "You must've had a long drive, late as you got here?"

"Yes," he responded. "I'm from Northern California, in Monte Vista. Thanks again for holding the reservation."

"No problem. I hope you're enjoying yourself. Everybody likes it here," she said. "Well, it looks like you got lucky. I have a cancellation, so you can keep the same room through Sunday. Is that all right?"

"Great, thanks."

"Sign in for me, will you?" she asked, sliding him the registration form. "I guess Ruby forgot to have you do it when she gave you the key. I've already extended the date to this coming Sunday."

"Sure," he answered, glancing at the form where he read, "Paradise Apartments, by the week or by the month." It was the best that Leona, his travel agent, had been able to do on such short notice. As he registered, Tom remembered the sign on the street: made from plywood painted yellow, and surrounded by green-painted palm fronds. Some Paradise.

THAT EVENING seven of them went out for pizza at the cute little place on the main drag — pizza and beer served on red-checked table clothes. Tina met Maggie on the corner between their places, and they walked toward the restaurant together.

"So where's the dreamboat?" Maggie asked, right off the bat.

"He has a meeting, tonight," Tina answered, knowing exactly whom she meant.

"What kind?" was the response.

"What kind of what?"

"Meeting. What kind of meeting?"

"Oh, some business thing."

"What does he do?" Maggie continued to grill her.

"Something in aerospace."

Wasn't that what he said? She tried to recall, but found that she couldn't remember any of the details, not for sure. There had been something about the moonshot. Tina became even more irritated, now, simply because she didn't know for certain. In fact, what did she really know about him at all?

Maggie finally took the cue from Tina's one-and-two word answers and started talking about something else — herself — which was Maggie's favorite subject anyway. They continued walking toward the restaurant together, meeting up with the others along the way. Apparently each of the originals had called and invited someone else and so on. Only two in the growing group were a committed "couple," so Tina did not feel like a fifth wheel. It was just a group of friends, out for something to eat.

Whoever ended up in front, leading the group, chose to take the short cut down the alley. Tina normally did not and would not have come this way just because of the bar. She found herself looking at the sign above the rear entrance for Pandora's Box, a topless joint, the shame of the neighborhood and all of The Shore.

"Don't you just love this place?" someone up front commented.

"Well, it's colorful, anyway," came the answer.

Tina thought that she would hardly refer to Pandora's that way. The bar had been in and out of court for years — for serving minors, fist fights in the parking lot, drunks passed out in backyards or peeing on fences, immoral and lewd acts. Its neon sign stuck out like a glow-in-the-dark tee-shirt would in a church, blinking off and on, on and off. The neon tubing outlined the real artwork of the sign — a semi-clad female, wearing only a scarf around the hips, knotted above one thigh, her hands covering and cupping a generous bosom. Obviously a Greek woman, like her namesake, because of the letters on her headband: Sigma Epsilon Xi. Very original, that one. As someone once joked, Pandora's had class, third class (Ha, ha), but class!

"I think the place is disgusting," Sue said.

"Well, it doesn't do much for equal rights," said Maggie, "but it sure keeps the men stirred up."

Most of the group joined in the laughter, except for Tina, who did not see much of anything funny about the place. The transient nature of The Shore seemed to protect the bar. No one took complaints by the permanent residents seriously. Any referendum was soundly defeated by a coalition of bar merchants who offered free drinks to students who would vote, an unwise political move that had gotten one place closed, but nothing ever changed. The moral right always lost by a surprisingly large margin.

Tina would not have chosen to walk by this rear, alley entrance to the place, unless it were early in the morning, before it opened. You never knew who or what you might meet. Tonight, with the whole group having her in tow, she didn't worry about it. The swinging door was propped open to let in some of the evening air, but it also let out some of the noise and loud music. The dark inner curtain was cracked just enough to place some light on the two figures standing in the entry. One was Tom.

It was dark in the alley, but, at that moment, she would swear it was Tom, standing there with one of the dancers, still in her costume. She was running her fingers across his chest, familiar and possessive. The woman glanced inside, nodded, and turned back to give the man a quick kiss, before disappearing again into the bar. Then the man — Tom — stepped out onto the concrete. Only at that moment did Tina realize just how drunk the person was.

He did not look at the group but staggered, reached out for the wall, got his bearings, and then took off down the alley, moving away from the street and behind them. Controlled, determined, but definitely drunk. The whole scene took only a few seconds to play out, but the details, colors, lighting, expressions, all seemed frozen in a moment of time, like a little picture inside one of those Disneyland glass globes — topless dancer and mystery man. Shake the scene and see it snow around them as they touch and kiss, on and on, eternally.

"Tina, are you coming?" Sue asked, pulling her back to the moment and back to the group.

"Sure, I'm here."

Tina turned and followed them, full of strange feelings. Tom had said that he was going to a meeting tonight. Some meeting! she thought. She had only known him for two days, but seeing him this way really shocked her. Almost immediately, she started doubting her own senses. *Maybe the man just looked like Tom*, she told herself. It was pretty dark in that alley. Yet she continued to replay the scene, the touch, the kiss, the familiarity. Obviously, they knew each other well — very well, indeed. The man was more than a customer who had given her a big tip. The touch and kiss had far more history behind them than just a single evening.

Tina replayed the scene several more times as the group walked the four buildings to the restaurant. The farther from the bar, the more confused she became. It had been dark in the alley, and she had been quite a ways from the back door, she remembered, but before she could reach any resolution, she was inside the pizza place, with the noise, the smells and the people. Fun and laughter, except she wasn't feeling jovial.

TOM GOT TO THE MEETING quite early, well ahead of time, because he was unfamiliar with the area. He simply followed instructions in the directory, but as it turned out, he could have left half-an-hour later and been on time. Still and all, he hated to be late, so this was the price he paid. When he walked into the room, there was no one present, but he could hear noises from the kitchen. Tom looked in and found a blondish-brown-haired man with a beard and pony tail struggling with a large coffee pot, trying to get the stem into the hole.

"Hey, how ya doin?" the man called when he saw Tom. "Be with ya in a minute. This damn pot always drives me crazy."

Tom gave him a hand, and soon, between the two of them, they had the coffee brewing.

"Thanks," the man said. "Are you new here?"

"Yes," Tom answered him. "First time at this meeting."

"My name's Russ," the man said, offering his hand. "Radical Russ they call me."

"I'm Tom. Glad to know you."

"Likewise. Are you new to the program?"

"Pretty new. Just about a year."

"Hey, that's great," said Russ. "Are you visiting the area, or what?"

"For now. I live up north, but I may be moving here soon."

"Super. Here, give me a hand putting out the coffee cups, and I'll show you around. Introduce you to some of our members. They oughta start drifting in any time now."

Tom was glad to have something physical to do. It helped him not to be nervous. By the time the meeting was ready to start, he had made several new friends. The first people to arrive were a couple, Martha and Martin, or "Marty" as he wanted to be called. They were married, having met in the program, which Tom learned from the bubbly Martha within the first minute he knew them.

"Just call us the M-and-M twins," Martha said, grinning up at him, she being on the small size, a bouncing bundle of energy — a little chubby, perhaps, and busty, with a rounded, smiling face.

Tom shook hands with Marty, who just rolled his eyes, and said, "Don't mind her, she can't help it." But Martha would have none of it, demanding a full hug, instead.

"They do hug up north, don't they?" she asked, teasing him.

"Sure. I'm just not used to it, I guess," Tom said. "My home group is pretty serious, and it's a men's stag meeting, on top of it." It had taken him a while to get used to all the hugging in the program, his own family being very standoffish, physically.

"Well," Martha told him, "this is Southern California. Get used to it. We hug first, then get serious afterwards."

She had a zest for life that was infectious, and everyone seemed to flock around her, drawing on her spirit. As it turned out, Martha and Marty were both older, returning students at the university, having started together after they were married. "We're going to graduate together, no matter how long it takes," Martha told him.

"Good luck," Tom said, happy to notice that they weren't kids but closer to his age, maybe older. When Tom mentioned that he might be starting school this next semester, she was delighted.

"Great, we have meetings on campus, too," Martha said. Then she introduced Tom to a dozen people, telling them he was definitely going to start graduate work at the university — as she put it, "a done deal." Part of Tom hoped she was right.

ONCE AGAIN, Tina found herself sitting with a group of her friends but feeling totally alone. After the food was delivered, Lisa broke away from Bill long enough to talk with Tina while nibbling on a slice of pizza.

"Where've you been, Tina?" she asked.

"Just around, I guess."

"I missed you on the beach today," Lisa said.

"I was there," Tina answered, realizing that Lisa had been so engrossed in Bill that she wouldn't even remember seeing Tina farther down the beach with Tom. But isn't that the way it's supposed to be, Tina asked herself, when you're in love? All wrapped up in each other?

Lisa shrugged her shoulders, almost in answer, her mouth full of pizza, then turned back to her boyfriend, effectively cutting Tina off from that end of the table, not maliciously, but simply because Lisa and Bill's conversation was so definitely private. Tina looked in the other direction just in time to catch Maggie glancing away. Tina was sure that Maggie had been watching her just the second before, but Maggie not only looked away, she started talking to Sue across the table, talking in a low confidential tone that excluded Tina just as effectively as she was being ostracized from the other end of the table.

What am I doing here? Tina asked herself, partly wishing she were with Tom and out of this situation, but also partly wishing she'd never met him — especially if he really was the man in the alley. Life had been so much simpler a few days ago. Hadn't it? As she sat there toying with her salad and pizza, she again replayed the scene in back of Pandora's. It couldn't have been Tom standing there — it just didn't make sense that he would tell her he had a meeting, then go to a bar — yet the more she thought about the scene, the more his face became locked into it. Tom and the Topless Dancer, kissing on and on. Tina excused herself early and walked home alone, her hands thrust deeply into the pockets of her windbreaker. She'd never felt so alone in all her life.

She thought of calling her friend, Grace, in Paris but knew it would be too late over there. Maybe tomorrow?

"I'M TOM, an alcoholic from Monte Vista," he said, introducing himself to the group when the leader asked for visitors to the area.

He was greeted with a, "Hi, Tom," said in unison, and by a round of applause that was both familiar and pleasant, a warm, welcoming gesture.

It had been four or five days since his last AA meeting, too long for his comfort zone. If he did move here, he would have to find a new home group. Beginning from scratch, again, just like the first time he walked in almost a year ago. Some of his friends in the program back home had warned him that he was trying to do too much, too early. Going back to school full-time would be a big step. But his sponsor, Wayne, had just listened to what he was saying, and nodded. He would have his sponsor's support, no matter what, as long as Wayne knew he was working the program. Unconditional support. What a concept!

As he waited for the meeting proper to begin, Tom let his mind explore the events that led to his being here. Getting sober had been difficult, far more difficult than he would have thought possible. He drank his way through college, just like all his friends. Of course, that might say something about his choice of friends back then. The drugs in Vietnam had been good, even necessary, he once believed, but he quit them with ease. After his discharge, it was the drinking that kicked him, and kicked him hard. He had to drink to keep the memories at bay. Otherwise there would be no sleep and a miserable time at work the next day. It was a balancing act. Sober but no sleep. Or hungover but rested, sort of rested anyhow. That hell had lasted for almost two years, until the company sent him in for treatment. Thanks to the unit in St. Luke's, he had gotten his start in Alcoholics Anonymous. It saved his life.

He had walked in here, tonight, not knowing a single person in advance. Now he knew several people by name. One of them was a young man named Brian, also new to the meeting, who was planning to start school in a week as a freshman. Brian was sitting right in front of him. A thin, dark haired boy with a ready smile, Brian was eighteen-years old, and next week he would have two years of sobriety. It was a different world with kids having to get sober in their teens. Tom wondered if he would be here next week to see Brian take his two-year cake? A big part of him hoped so.

The meeting began with the familiar readings, portions of The Big Book he had heard hundreds of times, now. As people began talking — "sharing" from the podium — Tom tried not to be critical of the meeting, but it was difficult, not because of anything they did or said, but because he was the stranger, that and because the podium always intimidated him. He knew from watching new people come into his own home group that it took time to fit in, time and patience. He had precious little of either one. As he listened to the sharing, however, he started to realize that many of the members here were students, even a couple of teachers. It made sense, of course, once he started looking around the room. This was a university town, after all. People were sharing about difficult classes, fear of failure, problems in trying to determine a major — many feelings he could understand.

Tom's own home group was older than this one and, on the average, more staid and conservative. Perhaps he would be able to fit in here, easier than he expected? Only one way to find out, he thought, as he put up his hand to be recognized, to take a chance on sharing in front of a new group. The leader pointed to him and nodded. Tom walked to the podium, took a deep breath and began.

ONCE AGAIN, the bath water was as hot as she could stand it. Relaxing, easing away the tensions of the day — a bath usually worked for her, but not this evening. Each time she gave in to the heat and the sensation of the water, her mind returned to the scene at Pandora's. Why can't I let it go? she wondered. Tom had seemed so nice, yet there he was with some topless dancer. A slut! Who knows? She might be a graduate student with two kids to support. Sure! Or his sister. That was just as likely. But he was drunk. That much was obvious. Tina did not like drunks, having had too much experience with them, her own father, for one. I hope the hangover is killing him, she thought, feeling very uncharitable. Right now, she thought, Tom was probably passed out on the beach, someplace. He'll be sorry, tomorrow.

Periodically, she added fresh hot water, whenever the tub turned cool. Eventually, she found herself shivering. How long had she lain there, up to her neck in hot, cooling, tepid, then cold water? Thinking without conscious thought, with just images — beaches, sidewalks, bars, shadows, and dancers? Time for bed. Yet she continued to lie there, thinking, but not thinking, all the while staring at the ceiling.

AFTER THE MEETING, Tom went with Radical Russ and several others to a local coffee shop where "the meeting after the meeting" continued for another hour or two. On the way into the restaurant, Russ pulled Tom to the side for a minute of private conversation.

"Hey, man. I heard what you said about the service, just getting discharged a couple of years ago. I saw a lot of action in Korea, so I know it can be difficult coming home. Were you in Vietnam?"

"Yes," Tom said, "two tours."

"Pretty rough," Russ said, as he pulled out a business card which he handed to Tom. "Maybe we can get together sometime and talk about it, if you like?"

"Sure," Tom answered him. "Maybe so."

"Okay. Give me a call — anytime."

"Thanks, Russ," Tom said, as he looked at the card. What was a middle-aged hippy with a pony tail doing with a business card? he wondered to himself, as they moved into a large booth. Before putting the card into his pocket, Tom learned that "Radical" Russ was really Russell Thornton, Attorney at Law and Counselor. In spite of his year's experience in the program, Tom was still a little surprised. You just never know whom you'll meet in AA.

As a visitor and a relative newcomer to the group, Tom was the focus of the conversation for a while.

"So what brings you to town, Tom," a man named Andy asked, "just a vacation?"

"More or less," he answered. "I have an interview at the university later this week."

"Are you a teacher?" a tall, blond woman named Lindie asked. Tom remembered from something she had said in the meeting that she was a retired teacher, herself.

"Not yet, but I may be soon."

"Good luck," she responded. "Let us know how the interview turns out. Maybe I can help."

Then he was off the hook for a while as their conversation turned to other matters. Everyone seemed to be concerned about a man named Frank who was back in the hospital, apparently with an ongoing health problem. Two or three people at his table agreed to meet at the hospital the next day to visit the man.

"Frank's one of the real old-timers in this area," a woman named Kay leaned over and explained to him, even while she continued listening to the others. "He has spinal cancer. In remission for a long time, but it doesn't look good now."

Once again, Tom was struck with the power of the program — everyone pulling together, helping each other through all the good and bad spots. He didn't know Frank, but he could sense how much the man meant to everyone at the table. Tom knew he was witnessing legitimate love and caring. He looked around at the group. Two of the men were in business suits, long-sleeved shirts and ties. Others were just wearing tee-shirts. One of the women was dressed in what had to be an expensive designer outfit, while sitting right next to her was a younger woman in cutoff jeans. Where else could you find something like this? It was a true democracy. Tom had come to Golden Shore alone, knowing no one, yet now he had several new friends. He felt himself being washed over by a wave of gratitude, for himself, for everyone at the table, and for a dying man he hadn't even met, but someone he already felt he knew.

LATER IN BED, Tina tossed and turned, never quite sure if she were awake or asleep. When she replayed the scene, she could no longer see his face, Tom's face from the beach that very day, or the man's face from the bar that evening.

Instead, she saw her father's face, kissing another woman, not her mother. It was one of her clearest memories from childhood. The kiss was not under the lights of Pandora's, but under the light of the laundry room just off the kitchen at home, as the couple stood there pressed against each other, framed in the doorway. Her parents were having a party, and Tina had gotten up for a drink of water. There was history behind that kiss, too. She sensed it, then, and knew it now. Who was the woman? She had to be a friend of Tina's parents for her to be there at the party, but Tina could not remember the name. She thought it was something like Lillian or Lilith, but neither seemed right. Her mother would know. In Catholic grade school, she learned the bible story of David and Bathsheba, so that became the way Tina thought of the woman — Bathsheba, the woman who took her father away. Her father's name was David, too. Even without knowing the woman's real name, Tina could and did remember her face and had remembered it, off and on, for years.

Now she saw the face again, and it was the face of the topless dancer at Pandora's, the self-same face. But how could that be? Almost fifteen years apart? She saw them kissing, again, under the neon light of the bar sign. It was the face of her father and the face of the neighbor, now becoming the faces of Maggie and Tom, kissing. Time and memory merged, confusing her. Hadn't they torn down Pandora's, several years ago? Not just closed it, boarding up the doors and the windows, but torn it down to the ground, in some communal act of rage?

Nothing was making sense, now. Tina knew it was late — the middle of the night, in fact — but she chose not to look at the clock. She could sleep in, tomorrow morning, just relax. There was less than a week left until classes began again. The last thing she remembered was the back of a man's head, standing in the dim light of an alley, as he kissed a Greek-looking woman, or maybe she was Hebrew, her hair braided with silver ornaments. Tina tried to see the man's face, but just as he turned, she fell asleep.

Chapter Three: Wednesday

THE KNOCKING ON THE DOOR WAS FIRM, not loud, but insistent. Suddenly, far too suddenly, Tina was wide awake, looking at the clock. Good grief! It's almost ten, she thought, getting up and pulling a robe around her. She hadn't slept this late in months. But why was she answering a knock when she wasn't even dressed? Partly out of guilt, she supposed. People should be up and about at this time of day. Tina undid the security chain and opened the door, only to look out and find him standing there — Tom.

Stunned, she said, "Hi."

Smiling, he held up a bag from the bakery. "I brought breakfast with me."

Like a sleepwalker, she stood aside and let him in. Realizing that her mouth was hanging open, she made an effort to close it. What was going on here? Tina asked herself. Only too late did the scene at Pandora's come rushing back, and along with it her decision to steer clear of this man. Tom seemed to be in such good spirits that it took him a minute to realize she had just awakened. Judging by his late reaction, Tina thought she probably looked like a walking zombie, but how could this man look so alert when he had been so drunk the night before?

"Really, I'm sorry," he said. "I just assumed you'd be up." He apologized again and started to leave, but she insisted that he stay, out of her own curiosity if nothing else. This could not be the same man she saw bouncing off the alley walls last night.

"No, please stay. It's all right," she answered. "I'm usually up long before this." And it was all right because Tina wanted to see this one through, no matter what. She had to know if she'd been dreaming about the night before, or if she were just losing her mind.

"Are you sure?" he asked.

She nodded yes.

"What about dishes and glasses?"

She pointed to the cupboards on the right of the sink, and then went back into the bedroom to get dressed after first locking the door, something she seldom if ever bothered doing.

Only taking time to wash her face and run a comb through her hair, she debated about pants and a blouse, but decided to put on the dry bikini and a cover up. What now, a quick breakfast and then off to the beach? As if nothing had happened? She silently asked these things of her reflection in the mirror. Getting no answer, she stared at herself for another minute, then turned and walked out of the room, heading for the kitchen. She was curious, to say the least, but nervous, too, even a little frightened. It was too early in the morning for this. But it wasn't early. It was late. Everything was relative, she supposed. In just two days, major portions of her world had been thrown into flux.

Tina walked into the kitchen, full of misgivings, so much so that the scene she entered struck her as doubly strange. Tom had set the table and poured two glasses of the orange juice he had brought with him. He was standing in front of the coffee pot, with his hand holding the scoop poised above the basket, a serious, quizzical look on his face. Tom must have heard her enter because he turned to look at her.

"Are four scoops okay?" he asked.

"Yes," she answered, mechanically, "that's what I use."

Why, she wondered, did seeing Tom in her own kitchen in such a domestic pose please her so, in spite of all her misgivings? For one thing, because she'd asked him in, he hadn't broken in like Ed, but it was something more — his attitude, too, the way he was. Tom wasn't invading her space. He acted like a guest who just wanted to help out. She smiled when an irrational picture of Tom in a frilly apron flashed before her eyes. Then, still smiling, she moved to help him finish up the breakfast preparations. Once again, she supposed, all things were relative.

"HOW DID YOUR MEETING GO last night?" Tina asked him, carefully, not wanting to seem obvious or to appear to be prying.

"Fine," he answered, without explanation of any sort.

"Did you get plenty of sleep?" *Now, what kind of a question was that?* she asked herself. "I mean did the meeting run late?"

"No," he answered her, "not particularly. I've already been up and gone running on the beach this morning. Can't seem to sleep past sunrise, anymore, haven't since the service."

"I'm usually up early, too. Except for this morning," she said, putting cream cheese on a bagel. "Do you take anything in your coffee?"

"Just black, thanks."

How could he be up at dawn, running on the beach, if he had been so drunk the night before that he could hardly stand up? What a constitution, she thought, stifling a yawn. Once again, the scene at the bar played itself in her mind. Was it he? Had the whole thing been a — been a what? Had she imagined it or dreamed it, the face of her father and the woman, Bathsheba, from her childhood? The pain of that memory transferred itself into the present.

What was she doing breaking bread with a man she had just met two days before, someone she had seen kissing a topless dancer last evening? Should she just ask him, outright? Was that you I saw last night, in the alley, with the half-naked Grecian? How do you ask a question like that? Especially of someone who looked so refreshed, ready for the day? It just could not have been him. Damn it. Damn it all. Nothing was making sense. The sound of another bagel popping out of the toaster startled her back to this kitchen, here and now. She made a vow to go by the Italian restaurant sometime today, just to see if the bar was still there, four doors down. One way or another, that would prove something — wouldn't it?

"I'm sorry for waking you," he said, apologizing again. "But I've got an appointment this afternoon and evening with one of the professors at the university. I wanted to get an early start on the day."

"What's the appointment about?" she asked, when he did not continue right away.

"A teaching job. I'm to meet some of the faculty and be grilled by them, like a trout on a skewer," he said, smiling in a way that suggested he was not looking forward to the experience. "But I have some questions for them, too. Hopefully the answers will help me decide."

Decide what? she wondered. Why did he always seem to talk in code? Was he really going to teach at the university, then, at her school? She started to ask, but he had moved on to another subject, already starting to make plans for the rest of the time they would have together. Later, she would ask. He made the interview sound so ominous, and intense. But then everything about him was intense, or had been. Something was different about Tom this morning, something had changed since yesterday. He was freer, more open, and he smiled a lot more.

"WHAT'S A PALINDROME?" she asked, later, still amazed at how animated he had become, overnight.

"MADAM I'M ADAM, you know a word or phrase that reads the same way backwards and forwards. Like the name Otto is O-T-T-O both ways."

How had that come up? Tina wondered. She watched as he sketched several words and phrases that were palin — what was it? Palindromes. Something to do with his being an English major and enjoying word games, puns and the like. Allegory and symbolism. She remembered the terms from high school English, one of her favorite subjects back then. In college, her majoring in Education had taken up most of her course work, so far, along with the usual general ed requirements. It was not so much what he said that held her attention as the way he said it. He was a born teacher, passionate and in love with his subject. It pleased her to see this in him, and it made her respect him for the passion.

She felt the same way about teaching. Ever since she could remember, she had wanted to teach children, but for almost as long, she had felt guilty about choosing such a career, as if it did not matter, somehow, was not important in the larger scheme of things. Overheard conversations, snide, ignorant comments, condescending smiles — she had experienced all these from family, friends and classmates, as if a woman chose teaching for lack of anything better to do, like getting married and having children. What had he asked?

"I'm sorry," she said. "I was daydreaming. What did you say?"

"I just asked about your major."

"Education." A chill ran down her arms. Had he read her thoughts? "I'm going to be an elementary teacher."

"I know. You told me yesterday. I was just wondering if you were through with your credential courses?"

"All except for student teaching. I'll be doing that first thing this fall semester," she added. "In a week, really, just down the street here at the local grade school."

"My mother was a teacher," he responded. "She loved it. You said you're a senior?"

"Yes."

Past tense about his mother, Tina noticed. She must have died, then. The way he said the words carried a sadness, but he did not pause to explain. Instead, he told her that he was seriously thinking about teaching as well.

"I'm up for a special teaching fellowship in English at the university. They have a last-minute opening because of an illness. If I'm accepted, I'll get to teach some of the same courses I just took for the MA. A nice opportunity, but it'd be going right from the proverbial fire into the frying pan, with hardly a rest. I'd also begin doctoral work at the same time, in just a week. Assuming, of course, that I even get the offer, first, or choose to accept it, second."

"What else would you do?" she asked.

"Stay where I am," Tom explained. "I'm on vacation from an aerospace subsidiary up north, TST — Time and

Space Technologies, if you've heard of them? I've worked there since getting out of the service. They've given me one week at the beach, to make up my mind."

Once he started talking, he could not seem to stop, but Tina was happy to listen. She had learned more about him in the past half-an-hour than in two full days, previously.

"This week I get interviewed," he continued. "Should I accept the offer or turn it down? I just don't know. The PhD is a long haul. I think that I would enjoy university teaching, but my real goal is to write. Academics would be a base, a structure, while I see about the writing. Aerospace pays well. I just don't know if I can cut back to living on an academic stipend."

She knew, just by watching him. It was absolutely crystal clear! Of course he could. Not once in two days had he mentioned anything really scientific. Nothing about the job or the calculations, just the excitement of the moon shot. Perhaps it was all classified, and he could not talk about it? No. That was not it. When he talked about writing and English, he was animated, alive, in love with the subject. She could tell him what to do, right now, just by watching him. But he was not asking, really. He was just talking, using her as a sounding board, exploring options as he talked, his hands making motions on the table. She did not resent his distraction. She found it rather nice, in fact, even comfortable, making her feel needed.

"I'm sorry," he said. "I didn't mean to rattle on like that."

"Don't be silly. I enjoyed it."

He looked flustered, as if he'd said too much, somehow. Revealed too many secrets. She really was pleased to hear of his plans. The idea that he might be teaching at the university and living here was suddenly intriguing.

ANOTHER GOOD DAY, she thought later, as they walked to the beach. They picked up something more to eat for lunch at one of the stands on the pier. Just simple hot dogs, with mustard and relish, Pepsis and potato chips. A perfect lunch for a perfect day. Gorgeous California weather, but always, somewhere in the back of her mind, was that picture from the night before of the man and the topless dancer, fading from moment to moment, but always there. It could not have been this man, this Tom. No one could recover that quickly, and yet last night she would have sworn it had been he, drunk in the alley.

"I thought I saw you last night around 6:00," she said, when she could stand the suspense and suspicion no longer.

"Where was that?"

"Downtown, near the pizza parlor."

"I'm not sure where that is, but at 6:00 I was getting dressed for the meeting, so it couldn't have been me."

He did not react as if he were covering up something. Just a simple no and a shrug as if she had been mistaken. It make her feel better.

In the early afternoon, they walked to the new library that had opened in The Shore. State of the art. Tina lived here and was embarrassed to admit that she didn't even know where to find the new building. The artwork and architecture were truly amazing. How had Tom heard about this place when she hadn't? Tina discovered that she still had a library card which just needed renewing. It had lapsed because all of her research was done at the university now.

Pleased with herself, she checked out a couple of books that she would try to read before the semester began.

"Do you want to get a book or two?" she asked Tom, offering to let him use her card.

"No, thanks. I'd like to, but not until I know for sure about the move. I'll get a card then."

Tina watched him as they roamed about the library, following their individual whims. When he moved on to another area, she walked over and checked the shelves he'd just left. Tom had been looking at a section on poetry, Shakespeare and other writers of the Renaissance. One of the books he'd pulled out and inspected was Edmund Spenser's *The Faerie Queene*. She had never heard of it.

He left shortly afterward for his appointment, promising to come by her house in the morning, if she didn't mind, but still leaving her there, with two library books and a new card. What now? She couldn't go to the beach until she took the books home, so she headed back to her house. As she walked, the rest of the afternoon and the evening stretched itself out before her. A long, blank expanse. Twice, she turned to look behind her, having a strange feeling of being followed. Was she getting paranoid or what?

Tina knew her reaction had to do with last year's news, the horror of the Sharon Tate killings and that madman Charles Manson. How could anyone feel safe in times like these? Such violence. Just two years ago, Martin Luther King and Bobby Kennedy had been assassinated. Tina knew people who locked their doors now, when they never had before, she being one of them. Manson was the scariest. How could all those young women allow themselves to be hypnotized by the man? She had seen one picture of Manson that clearly showed his eyes. They were hypnotic, but still ...

all the girls said they loved Charlie, as they called him, loved the man. Tina shuddered and looked behind her once more. She felt safe when she was with Tom. She wished he were here now.

She had known Tom for only three days and missed him already. What if he accepted the teaching position at the university? What then? He would be going to school right here, in her town, at her school, in the English department. Yesterday, the thought would have pleased her. Maybe even an hour ago. Now, as she entered her quiet house, she didn't know. She still hadn't completely resolved the night before at Pandora's Box. How could it have been Tom, standing there? Yes or no? Maybe she didn't want to know. Not right now. She could just stay home and read. Or she could try to locate some of her girlfriends. Or she could call her mother to see if she were free for dinner and a movie. Tina felt a sudden need for family. It was only a forty-five minute drive. Why not call?

"Hello." Her mother answered on the second ring.

"Hi, mom, it's Tina."

"How are you, dear?"

"Fine. Do you feel like going to a movie tonight?"

"That would be fun. What time?"

"You tell me."

"How about five o'clock? I think there's a double feature tonight."

"Okay. See you then."

Tina felt good about the call after she had hung up. She tried to see her mom every week, or every two weeks, at least, and they talked on the phone, but they still lived in separate worlds, and they had ever since her parents divorced. Not that she took her father's side — anything but that — after all, he had left them, but her mother was fragile and needy. She was doing fine these past few years, and they did better together as mother and daughter, but only because Tina limited the time she spent with her mother.

Family, Tina thought, so important when you don't have it, taken for granted when you do.

AFTER GETTING CLEANED UP, Tom decided to do a little shopping, just so he would have something to eat in the apartment. There was still time before he needed to leave for the campus, so he walked the block to the local market. Since their floorplan was new to him, Tom was a little distracted as he moved up and down each aisle hunting for his few items. At first he did not recognize Maggie ahead of him until she turned in profile. He couldn't help but admire her figure. Dark, tawny skin, well-tanned and conditioned. Beautiful auburn hair. She was wearing an open blouse over a bikini.

As Tom moved down the aisle toward her, Maggie was stretching to reach a box on the top shelf, but she came up an inch or two short.

"May I?" Tom asked, reaching toward the box of cereal she was after.

"Well, hello," she said. "Tom, isn't it? Just when I needed a big strong man to rescue me."

They moved down the aisle together, making small talk. It was obvious to Tom from the stuff in their baskets that they had begun at different ends of the store and would be separating at the end of this section.

"Did you go to the beach today?" she asked, looking up at him as she reached down for a bottle of cooking oil.

"Yes, earlier," he answered her, aware that she knew exactly what she was doing by bending over in front of him. "Tina and I went down for a couple of hours."

"Can I borrow your pen?" she asked, after standing up.

Tom looked down at his pocket having forgotten that he'd put a ballpoint pen there. Scientific habit, he supposed. "Oh, sure," he said, but before he could start to reach for the pen, she plucked it from his pocket, her fingers caressing his chest as she pulled the pen free.

"Here's my number," she said writing the digits on a roll of paper towels he was going to buy.

"I'll only be here a week," he told her, as if that were an answer.

"Give me a call, anyway," she said, shrugging. "What can it hurt? Nothing ventured, nothing gained." She returned the pen to his pocket, carefully patting it back into place, her touch warm and electrifying. "Thanks," she said, giving the pen one last adjustment.

"Anytime," he said, automatically.

In a seemingly unconscious gesture, she took the two lower points of her open blouse-front and tied them in a knot under her bikini bra, but instead of covering her in any appreciable way, the knotting actually served to lift and frame her breasts, accentuating them even more.

"Good to see you, Tom. Call if you like."

"Nice running into you, Maggie."

Tom watched as she walked away. Her suit was cut briefly enough that the dimples on her lower back showed above the line of her bikini bottom. Venus dimples, he remembered they were called. A very appropriate name, he thought. As her hips and buttocks swayed and flexed with her steps, the dimples remained fixed, like two eyes, staring back at him, hypnotically, as she moved off down the aisle.

BACK IN HIS APARTMENT, Tom unpacked and stored the two bags of groceries. As he mechanically went about the chore, his mind raced ahead to the next few days. He wondered what he would find on campus. There was no way to predict it. He would just have to wait and see what developed.

Tom tore open the paper towels and started to toss the wrapper into the trash can in the corner. His eye caught some writing, so he paused to look. It was the phone number, Maggie's number. Tom shook his head in admiration, as he formed a mental picture of her in the grocery store.

She's a beautiful woman, he thought, and well aware of her effect on men, but what kind of a friend could she be to make an offer like that to someone her girlfriend was — was what? Dating? Is that what he and Tina were doing? It was as good a term as any, he supposed.

Still half-tempted to keep the number, Tom opened his hand and let the paper drop into the small trash can. That's how I used to treat women, he thought, like Kleenex. Use them and toss them away. A few years ago, when he was still drinking heavily, he would have kept the number and called it, first chance. *Good grief,* Tom thought, *by this time he would have hit on Maggie already.* But not now, so what did that make him? A sudden Puritan? Yes, Maggie was beautiful, that much was obvious, but loyal she was not, and loyalty was something Tom valued. On top of everything else, Tom knew he was a different person than he'd been, as he now traveled a narrower road. No one said that staying sober would be easy, he thought, taking one last glance at the phone number before turning and walking away.

AS TOM HEADED for the campus, he thought about Dr. Masback, the man who had set all of this in motion. They first met when Masback taught a summer class in Tom's college up north, coming in as a visiting professor. After the first required paper, the professor asked Tom to stay after class.

"Have you considered going on beyond the master's degree?" the man said to him, seemingly interested.

"Not really."

"You should," Masback told him, handing back Tom's paper. "This is good work, original work."

"Thanks," Tom said, feeling truly complimented.

After that, they had become friends, staying in touch during the previous year as Tom finished up his course work for the MA degree. Then just a week ago, Masback had called Tom to tell him about the sudden opening at his university. Would Tom be interested?

Well, that's what he was here to find out. Following the directions Masback had given him over the phone, Tom pulled his car into a parking lot on the upper campus. A guard in the kiosk motioned him in after checking to see if his name was on the master list on his clipboard.

"Who is it you're seeing?" the guard asked.

"Dr. Masback, in English," Tom told the man, knowing that his host's name was probably right there on the list. The guard was being doubly careful. The security reminded Tom of a military base. Ironic, he thought, that you would need guards to keep people out of a public university.

"Okay," the man said, "you can park anywhere marked Visitor."

"Could you direct me toward the Humanities Building?" Tom asked, leaning out of the window.

"Right there," the man said, pointing toward a large building in the distance. "English is on the Third Floor."

"Thanks," Tom said, then drove into the lot, passing under the raised wooden arm of the blockade.

He parked the car, got out, and headed toward his appointment. As he walked across the campus, Tom saw a man in fatigues, speaking to a sparse crowd. As he got closer, Tom realized that the man was exhorting several students to burn their draft cards. Except for his long blond hair, the man could have been a poster model for the military. He was wearing the insignia of a unit that Tom recognized from Vietnam, the 101st. Tom's own group had done a joint mission with men from that same division. This guy had seen combat, plenty of combat — Tom could sense it by watching the way he moved — yet here he was, urging students to burn their draft cards. *What was going on here?* Tom asked himself. Their eyes met across the ten yards that separated them. Tom was on the sidewalk, while the man in uniform was standing on a concrete base which supported a huge, free-form metal structure, something resembling a palm frond growing straight up, out of the ground. Tom felt himself stand just a little taller, almost coming to attention in the presence of the man's uniform. Tom knew he still walked with the traces of a military posture though he had finally learned to relax a little in normal circumstances. The man continued to address his audience while staring at Tom. Like two male dogs meeting on a street, they recognized each other, saw each other as soldiers, as warriors.

"Hell, no. We won't go," the man said, looking right at Tom.

"Hell, no. We won't go. Hell, no. We won't go," the audience repeated, picking up the chant.

Tom felt himself stepping out in time to their chant, as if to a march. He didn't like the feeling — as if he were supporting the words by walking in time to them. He tried to alter his pace, until he realized the soldier was deliberately timing his chant to Tom's steps. Tom knew he was being mocked, in some way that he didn't fully understand. Why would this man, a veteran, act in such a contemptuous way?

"Hell, no. We won't go. Hell, no. We won't go."

Tom stopped in place, continuing to stare at the man. The whole situation was a rag-tag joke, Tom knew, yet he was deadly serious in his reaction. One man in uniform, two or three young students supporting him, half-heartedly, while a dozen others looked on — this was the whole extent of the demonstration, yet Tom was frozen in place, staring at the man.

"Hell, no. We won't go. Hell, no. We won't go." For a minute or two longer, the chanting continued while Tom and the soldier looked at each other. Finally, the other man held up his arms for silence. Tom felt himself tensing for a confrontation, but the man did not challenge him. Instead, he turned away from Tom and began talking to the small group in front of him. He never looked back in Tom's direction. Eventually, Tom started moving up the path, again, with a final glance at the other man.

It was over. In another minute, Tom had passed out of range. He could no longer hear the speaker. Continuing on towards the Humanities Building, he carried with him the image of a Vietnam veteran, urging students to burn their draft cards. Tom had expected to see such things on this campus, but he hadn't been prepared for the soldier. The man had seen combat. How could he be here, leading a demonstration?

All the way up the hill, Tom thought about the man. All the way into the department offices, he carried the memory of a man in uniform urging students to rebel against their government. The secretary in the English Department directed Tom to Dr. Masback's office. The professor was expecting him.

"Tom, good to see you, again" he said, offering Tom his hand.

"You, too, professor."

"Did you get parked all right?" Masback asked him.

"Yes, the parking went fine. The guard said you'd arranged everything in advance. Thanks."

"No problem."

As they moved through the department halls, Tom was introduced to several people.

"Pleased to meet you, Professor," he said to one.

"Yes, Doctor, my pleasure," he told another.

Tom hated this part of the process, the introductions and inspections, but he had learned long ago to hide his reactions. By nature an introvert, now, ironically, by a possible career change, he could find himself standing in front of whole classes, veritable rooms full of students. As they walked down the halls, Tom imagined himself in this setting, on a regular basis. He liked the idea. Hallowed ivy walls. Ideas being treated with the respect usually reserved for corporeal beings. He had seen more than enough of the real world. Perhaps he could do with some time spent in the world of ideas, academia? The thought was arousing, exciting and intriguing. Just as long as it wasn't a hideout, a retreat into some ivory tower?

Tom was led into a small, narrow conference room, adjacent to the department library. Waiting for him were The Committee and several graduate students. The questions began even before he sat down.

"Hi, Tom. I'm Bill Crawford. Your field is the Renaissance, then?"

"Yes. Especially non-dramatic."

"You've written some on Spenser, I understand?"

The experience soon took on a sense of deja vu. Time warp. It was combat all over again, except that the choice of weapons here consisted of ideas, opinions, theories, and disciplines. Tom and Professor Masback were right on time. Through the single window, Tom could hear bells beginning to chime, like a call to arms. For an instant, Tom saw the face of the man he'd passed on the walk over. He tried to forget the man, but, as the bells sounded, "Bong, Bong, bong, bong, bong," Tom heard, "Hell, no. We won't go."

He took a deep breath and forced the memory from his mind. As usual, his control was up to the task. The man in uniform faded away as Tom focused on the faces in the room. He was ready. He met the challenge of the next question, fending off the feint he predicted would follow. One of the graduate students jumped in. What was his motivation? Tom wondered. Had he been considered for this same position but then been passed over? Something in the student's appearance and rebellious demeanor reminded Tom of the soldier, again. For an instant, Tom felt the beginnings of a rage surge through him, but he suppressed the response. He knew the rage was directed at the stress of the situation and at the other man's wearing of the uniform, not at this student's sarcastic question. Tom disarmed the young man easily but left him with a sense of having legitimately and valiantly put forth a challenge. Masback was next, his question going to Tom's strength, his expertise. It was like rendezvousing with an ally in the field. After that, they moved in order around the table, parry and thrust. Question after question.

THE PHONE RANG, just as Tina was getting ready to head out the door. It was her friend, Anna.

"Hi, Tina," she said. "Do you want to go for a drink tonight? There's a small combo playing at the Sundowner."

"No, thanks," Tina said. "I'm going over to my mother's for a visit. Dinner and a movie. That kind of thing."

"Oh, sure," Anna said, sounding disappointed.

A drink? Tina thought, remembering what her friend has said. That was still a new idea. They'd had both turned twenty-one in the same month, and not that long ago. Being able to drink legally was still a novelty. Anna especially liked to hit the clubs and the bars. She was a good dancer and very sociable, but going into a bar alone was not something she liked to do.

"Maybe some other time?" Tina said, trying to ease the disappointment.

"Oh, sure. Have a good time with your mother."

They chatted for a little while longer about movies and what was happening with mutual friends, when Anna suddenly asked about Tom.

"How are things going with him?" Lisa asked.

"Good," Tina responded, guardedly, not willing to say more.

"Ed's sure been acting goofy, lately," Anna said. "Ever since you broke up with him."

"How do you mean goofy?" Tina asked.

"He still talks like the two of you are going to get back together again, once Tom's gone, that is."

"Tom doesn't have anything to do with it," Tina said, glancing at the clock. She would have to hurry, but she still wanted to know what Ed had said to her friends.

"Maybe so, but Ed thinks that's why you broke up with him."

"Not at all," Tina said, unwilling to explain in detail. It was too late to tell Anna about the break-in. She wouldn't understand now.

They talked for a minute longer. Anna decided that she might go down to the bar anyway or see if she could find someone else to go with her. They said their goodbyes, and Tina grabbed her purse and headed out the door. Why, she asked herself, did everything have to be so complicated?

LATER, THE COMMITTEE took him to a restaurant in the marina. A very nice one. Tom filed the information away. The department would pay, of course, but what did the choice of dinner houses tell him about their current budget? Was his offer negotiable? How much do professors make? he wondered. Assistant professors? Graduate assistants? He realized he had never asked. Tom filed that information away, too. In aerospace he was always conscious of salary. Everyone was. Supposedly top secret, salaries and raises were hotly debated and gossiped about. Your pay was your mark of success. Pay and position. Why had he never asked what his first full-time teaching job might pay? Because it didn't matter? Perhaps so. But why wouldn't it matter? He could think of two reasons. One, he wasn't really serious about this. Making such a change was too crazy an idea to take seriously. Returning to school at his age! Second, it really might not matter. If he got a chance to teach English and do some writing, perhaps the money was secondary? When the waitress came around for drink orders, Tom asked for his usual iced tea.

"Wouldn't you care for a cocktail?" Dr. Cheney, the department chair, asked him. "It's on the university, you know."

"No, thanks. I don't drink," he answered, simply, just as he had learned to do. Don't make a big deal out of not drinking, just refuse, politely.

"Probably just as well," she responded, glancing across the table at another of the committee members.

Tom had already spotted the man. A seasoned, full-professor of Victorian literature. He was a natty dresser even if the clothes were a little old-fashioned. The man had excused himself to go to the rest room as soon as they got to the restaurant, but first he had made a beeline for the bar and put down a quick shot. Tom had seen him stop for another shot on the way back from the john. When the drinks arrived, the professor called for a toast and managed to deliver it without any obvious slurring. He mentioned something about Tom's "oratorical splendor and rhetorical grandeur."

"Your health!" the man said, reaching across the table with his glass.

"Cheers," Tom responded, clinking glasses with him.

Their eyes met in a different sort of appraisal, one having to do with alcohol, not academics. The moment did not last, but the message was palpable, if untranslatable. Two drinkers. One of them sober. The professor sat down, heavily, looked at Tom once more and then turned to the man on his left.

Tom had gotten used to drinking events like these, more or less. Lord knows there were plenty of them at TST, where he worked. Time and Space Technologies. He was not fully comfortable in such situations but knew that he could get through them without craving a drink. He had done so, successfully, for almost a year. At this moment, thinking about his sobriety, Tom realized that one year ago today, he had been blindly drunk, on the verge of entering St. Luke's Hospital. In two weeks he would celebrate a one-year AA birthday. A new beginning. He looked around the table. A new beginning, indeed. Perhaps something completely new?

TINA ENJOYED the movies, a double feature of Peter Sellers frolicking about Paris as Detective Clouseau. They were being shown in an artsy little theater her mother liked. Never anything new or first run, unless it were foreign, but the movies were usually pretty good. The theater was set in a small shopping center just down the street. Several art galleries, craft shops and the like. The first film was the original *Pink Panther*, the second a later sequel. Even the sequel had come out a couple of years earlier, but neither she nor her mother had seen the films, so their age did not matter.

"The title is an oxymoron, a paradox in terms," her mother explained on the walk home. "My friend, Sylvia told me that — you've met her, dear? Pink is a feminine color. Panther a violent male animal. Hence the paradox."

"I think female panthers are probably just as violent as the male of the species," Tina said, instantly sorry when she realized how her mother could have taken the words.

"Yes, I suppose so," she answered, apparently having read nothing more into Tina's statement than a comment on the movie.

As they continued walking, her mother chatted on about the various cultural events coming up in her city. Tina only half listened.

Ironic, she thought. How could her mother talk about violence without remembering her own violent rages during her breakdown? Tina could remember them, the fear she felt as a child, the confusion. Not only had her parents divorced, but then her mother had gone crazy! And when her mother was at her worst, she was a screaming banshee of destruction. For a while, Tina had lived with her cousins. Difficult to believe, now, looking at her mother talking about art shows and community theater, a sweet, gentle person. Perhaps she did not remember? Perhaps the years of therapy had erased that portion of her life?

Tina imagined some giant, pink school eraser editing her mother's life, removing the things she wanted to forget. She listened as her mother rambled on, talking about the new movement in feminine consciousness. More power to her, Tina thought, happy that her mother had something to interest her. Pink power, she thought. A novel idea. After the divorce, her mother had gone face down in her pillow, for months it seemed. First the depressions, then the rages. Thank God, she could smile again. Her mother's name was Pearl. A pearl of great price, they always joked.

"How's the new priest working out?" Tina asked her mother.

"Quite nicely, dear. Father Leo really is very good, if a little on the young side." Still critical and negative, but now just out of habit it seemed.

The Church had kept her mother safe and secure, offering her a sanctuary of sorts. It had helped to save her sanity, given her a haven, but she let it protect her too much, Tina thought. Her mother had become the eternal martyr, the willing sacrifice. She was a middle-aged woman who would not leave the nest. But what was the harm, really? What was the harm? She looked happy. She was safe. But her mother would never remarry. Tina knew that, and, until just lately, thought she knew why. As a Catholic, she was still married to Tina's father, in the eyes of God and Church. It did not matter that he had been married and divorced twice more since. Religion was part of the reason, but not the whole explanation. Her mother had been hurt, badly hurt. So badly that most of her friends, now, were women, widows or divorcees like herself. *Maybe all of her friends were women?* Tina wondered. Her mother never mentioned a male name, other than her father's.

"Have you heard from your father, lately?" her mother asked.

"Just a card on my birthday. Three days late."

"He never was good with dates."

Always making excuses for him. Always and still. Forever long-suffering. Would it never change? Tina's great aunt had carried a torch for her ex-husband until the day she died. Sixty years after the divorce. And she wasn't even Catholic! At least her mother had a job now and a life, even if that life did not involve a man, except by proxy and memory. Again Tina thought of Tom and the curious blending of his face with her father's. Memory was a funny thing.

Tina and her mother made small talk over coffee at home, mostly family gossip. Home? That was a long gone house in the next county, back in Golden Shore. As an adult, Tina had chosen to stay in their home town, but both her parents had long since moved away. Every now and then Tina would drive by the old house, perhaps trying to maintain something? Recreate something? Her mother's apartment was not home, nor was her father's swinging singles condominium, especially not that place. Never. Tina had made her own home in The Shore, with a little help from the small trust left by her grandmother. Divorce was a mess. Worse if you were Catholic.

"You seem distracted, dear. Is everything all right?"

"Oh, sure. School starts up in a week. I'll be doing my student teaching."

"That's nice, dear."

Even her own mother didn't take her wanting to teach seriously. It was just something a woman did until she had a family and children of her own. Her mother would never marry again and yet she couldn't wait until Tina did. She could talk about the new feminism and still believe that a woman is not complete without a man. Was this a generational difference? That Tina could see these things and her mother could not? She would not mention Tom to her again, not tonight. That had been a mistake.

"Tell me about him, dear."

What did she know about Tom, really? "He's older and thinking about returning to school for a doctorate."

"In what field?"

"English." Was that it? Was that all she knew?

"Well, is he good looking? When do I get to meet him?"

Good grief! Her mother would probably invite him up for dinner and start buying baby clothes, given half a chance. Tina looked at her watch.

"I've got to go, Mom. It's really getting late."

"I'm not trying to pry, Tina," her mother said, stressing the *not*, but it was the tone, not so much as the phrasing to which Tina reacted. "After all, I am your mother. You could keep me informed."

It was the criticism, implied or direct, to which Tina reacted. It was the fault-finding that she remembered, preceding the yelling, that led to the punishing — all when she'd been a child, helpless to defend herself, verbally or physically. Against her will, Tina felt herself cringing, if only inside, expecting the hand to strike. Her mother hadn't struck her physically in years, but all the trigger reactions were still in good working order.

"I have my own life, mother," she said, her voice controlled and flat, though her heart was pounding.

"I'm sorry, honey," her mother said, truly chagrined, by the words, in part, but even more, by what she must've seen in Tina's eyes. Her mother dropped her glance. "I don't mean to pry," she said softly.

"It's okay, mom. I'm under a lot of pressure. I just overreacted."

They talked for a few minutes longer — just inconsequential stuff, to assure each other that they hadn't really argued or reacted in the old ways — and then they moved out of the kitchen to the front door. On the porch, they said goodby and kissed each other on the cheek.

"If you talk to your father, say hello for me. Bye, dear."

As she drove back to The Shore, Tina thought about her parents, thought about what they had done to each other and to their daughter. Maybe it had been a mistake to come here, tonight. Seeing her mother always triggered thoughts she did not like. Seeing her father was even worse. *Could someone like me have a good relationship, a happy marriage?* Tina asked herself. But of even more immediate a concern, could someone with my background teach children? More and more often, she was starting to wonder. Tina could not help the flood of thoughts that came as she followed the dotted line all the way home.

TOM AND PROFESSOR MASBACK took a long walk after the faculty dinner. Tom had really grown to appreciate the older man's friendship, his acting as a mentor.

"How's the writing coming, Tom?" he asked. "Any progress?"

"Not too much, lately. I still have the writer's block."

"Well, give it time. It'll work out."

The professor promised to call when they had determined the schedule for the next round of activities. There were still two other candidates to be interviewed, but he assured Tom that he had the inside track. Tom only half-listened as Masback went into the departmental politics. Whom to know. Who could help you. Who could hurt you. Tom liked the man, but also recognized his peccadilloes. He was a fine Medieval scholar, but someone who also loved the petty wars of departmental politics. A big fish in a little pond. Tom absolutely did not want to get involved in that part of academics, the politics. Would he have a choice?

Tom had caught Masback's correct usage: Whom to know. Who or whom? Subject or object? Whoever used whom anymore? English teachers did, he supposed, meaning that he would have to begin. Which side of the preposition would he choose? It was all relative.

"Over here is the new physics wing," Masback was saying, pointing out places as they passed. "The next building is Chemistry. Across the way will be the new Humanities Tower. Construction starts next year."

How appropriate, Tom thought, that it should be a tower. The proverbial ivory tower. As the professor continued talking, Tom thought about Tina. She mentioned wanting to be an elementary teacher, but it was more than a passing thought. It was really important to her. He would ask her more about it tomorrow. Ironic that they would meet by accident and both be thinking about going into teaching as careers. Tom wondered if grade schools had the same political problems as universities. He thought they probably did. It was just human nature.

Chapter Four: Thursday

THE NEXT MORNING, Tom walked down to the beach for his run. From far away, he mused, the earth looks like a blue marble, the milky-blue kind that was his favorite as a kid. At least that's what the astronauts say. And from even farther out, farther than the moon, what would it look like? A point of light, like a star? Then gradually, as it neared, a little bigger, with more definition, moving faster as it spun on, faster and larger, getting closer and closer. Thinking of this reminded him of a spectacular meteor shower he had seen during a summer camp in the mountains, as a child. Falling stars. Tom walked along the promenade, knowing the sun was just about to rise because of the changing light, the predawn light. Ahead he could see the moon, still bright but soon to be lost against the glory of the sun. We actually put a man up there, just a year ago, Tom thought, and he was a part of doing it, a small part to be sure, but something he would always remember.

"One small step for man, one giant step for mankind."

What a thrill that was! A moment of national rapture! Now the cutbacks have brought everything to a screeching halt. The cutbacks and the war's building up, more and more, in Vietnam. Would he be called back up? Called back to fight again? The thought ran cold, like a steel blade, all the way through him.

Service had been an obligation, a pay back for the schooling, but at the time he had actually wanted to go, convinced that it was right, just like they said. Now he wanted to stand up and scream — Get us out of there. Don't send any more kids. Enough. *How*, he wondered, *was he any different than the man who was leading the demonstration, yesterday?* Tom wanted the war to end, but he knew he would never stand there in uniform, urging students to burn their draft cards. No, he could never do that.

Against his will, he thought of Bruce. Celtic Bruce with the flaming red hair. They were friends, partners. Had gone through OCS together. Been assigned together. Been Advisors together. Been ambushed together. He had found Bruce the next day, neatly severed pieces of him scattered about in the clearing, his head the only part of him recognizable. His red hair was visible from the other side of the clearing. And what they had done to his head. God! No matter how often he thought of it, or how seldom, the scene would not fade. The blood. The ants. The smell. He was like a brother, but even closer. Bruce had been a part of him. He had been a part of Bruce. Some of his own body and soul were left behind in that clearing. He had thrown up, cried, gone on a killing rampage. But nothing helped. Not even the shrinks at the VA. The scene was still vivid, like a brightly-colored poster for a movie: brown, green, yellow and red, with the red running everywhere under the blinding sun.

He had already written some this morning. Thank God for the journals, without them he would have gone crazy. If he ever saw Miss Bunke again, he'd thank her for the journals she made them write in high school. A long-time habit now. A lifesaver. The journals and running, he thought, stretching in anticipation. Sometimes he just had to run, knowing that It was still back there, keeping pace, ready to pounce. Whatever It was? Nam? Death? Fear? It was It. Always had been, always would be. Christians called it the devil, he supposed. The word was too small. Lucifer had too romantic a ring. Satan was better. Beelzebub had a certain power to it.

Professor Masback had asked about the journals last night.

"Do you still have them?"

"Yes," he answered. They were in a storage locker, two states away. As far away as they could be and still remain in his possession.

"Could you use them, now? Could you write about your experiences from those journals?"

"I don't know," he answered, shaking his head.

What a question! He could not even touch them, let alone read them. Not now, anyway. Someday? Perhaps someday, but not soon. Bruce was in those journals. A whole year's worth of them had been lost in transit — five ledgers — but not the ones with Bruce in them. That much he did know. No. He could not reread and relive those journals, not yet.

Did he want to be a writer? Moot point. He was a writer already. Writers write. He had learned that from another English professor, not Masback, but Dr. Summerfield. Tall, distinguished, white hair, with a voice like a Shakespearian actor. Tom learned he was already a writer because he wrote, even if only for the sake of his own sanity, but did he want to be a published writer? That was the question, Horatio. Did he have anything to say that was not so private it still smelled of blood? He did not know. Masback was encouraging, liked his work, what little he had seen so far.

The man must have pulled some strings to get him admitted to the university so quickly, even making him eligible for the special, extended fellowship, because Tom did not have the full English literature credits to qualify. Just random courses here and there, mostly in the Renaissance. With math as a major, science had been an automatic minor, and English courses were just pushed aside, until the master's degree, but even half of those courses had been in tech-writing, paid for by his company.

Could he make a complete switch now? A career change? In mid-life? But if this was the middle of his life, and he was only twenty-eight, then he would be dead at fifty-six. He was still young, but by comparison, even that age sounded impossibly old. There were times in Nam when he knew he'd never see tomorrow. Yet here he was, still alive, thinking about going back to school. And why not? He'd always liked school. Even during the worst of his drinking, he had managed to get through the night courses and do well in them, surprisingly well. Would it be the same in doctoral courses? The students would be better, but, now that he was sober, so would he. The competition did not worry him. He had always thrived on competition. The ice man. Able to operate at peak efficiency in a crisis. No, it was not that kind of pressure that worried him. It was the pressure of trying to become a writer. Opening his own chest. Self-surgery. Writing from his heart when he did not know what was in there, not for sure. Or what it would do to him, if he let it out.

The sun was coming up now, bright, golden and promising. How could he feel negative, on a day like this? Such breath-taking beauty! Pristine. As if he were the first person in the history of the world to witness it. Yes, it was time to run. He could hear the feet behind him, coming closer. Perhaps he could gain just a little space on It today? Perhaps he could even get an answer from the universe?

"Tell me what to do!" Tom imagined himself hollering the words into the void. "Tell me what to do, do, do" they echoed back, but he knew the only answers would come from within himself.

He started off slowly, just a fast jog really, then gradually built the pace to an aerobic, distance-eating stride, one he could maintain for a long time. Longer if he had to. Maybe even forever?

Tom thought about the night before while he ran. Sometimes that was when he did his best thinking, when his body was totally distracted, occupied with the business of running. The offer was good, very good, judging by what he could gather from talking with other people, earlier. He came here partly knowing what to expect, but their package had been even better. He would be living on less than half of his current salary, and their medical plan would be through the clinic on campus, but still it could be done. The tuition would be covered as part of the package. Yes, it could be done. For a long time, he thought through the options, compared the benefits, weighed the consequences, all while he ran. Finally he slowed down and turned back.

Looking down at his bare feet, he watched the foamy water spurt up between his toes as he stepped along the ever-moving edge of the surf. At home, in the mountains, he could never run without shoes. Here the sand and salt water felt good on his skin, somehow natural, primitive. The water was cold but refreshing. As Tom cooled off from the run, he began to think of Tina. They had made no specific plans for the day because he had no way of knowing what would happen once he got on campus, yesterday. He had become the captive of the English Department now, their experiment for last evening and for whatever was to follow, today and the rest of the week. As he climbed the steps to his second floor rental, Tom thought about Tina again. So far he had not questioned their relationship. He enjoyed her company; she seemed to enjoy his. Why not? But a relationship was not something he could afford right now. Three days and already he was thinking of her in those terms. As he entered the apartment, the phone was ringing.

"Hello," he said, answering.

"Tom? This is Aaron Masback. Can you be here in an hour?"

"Yes, it'll be a little tight, but I think I could make it that fast. What's happening?"

"Just a chance to meet some more of our faculty before you present the paper. We're having a breakfast meeting on campus. Every vote counts, so I figured —"

"Sure. No problem. Is my parking slip still good for today?"

"All week."

"Okay. See you in an hour. Your office?"

"Fine. Thanks, Tom. Sorry to bother you so early. Hope I didn't wake you?"

"No, I've been up for hours. In fact, I just got back from running on the beach."

"Oh, to be young again. Well, I don't want to hold you up. Bye, Tom."

"Goodby, doctor."

As he showered and dressed, Tom realized he wouldn't be able to tell Tina about the call and the change in plans for the day. He didn't have enough time to stop by her place, besides which it was too early, especially after showing up when he did yesterday. Nor did he have her phone number, so he wouldn't be able to call, unless she were in the phone book. He would check later, on the campus.

TINA AWAKENED EARLY, much earlier than the morning before, she noticed with a wry smile. Fixing herself a simple breakfast, she tried to remember what plans she and Tom had made for the day. Pretty much a wait-and-see was the best she could recall. She didn't have his phone number, and as best she could remember, he didn't have hers either, but she was in the book, so that much could be solved pretty easily. Oh well, she thought, no matter what, Tom knew where she lived. Surely he would call or come by, once he knew his schedule at the school.

After cleaning up the breakfast dishes, Tina poured herself another cup of coffee and moved to the front room where she could enjoy the drink while looking at the ocean through the small picture window. It was not a panoramic view, but nice enough to please her. The sea was her source of strength and solace. Tina didn't call it meditation, but she supposed that described what she experienced during these quiet times. Such times were for praying and thinking, consciously or instinctively. The words didn't matter. Answers would come, with or without specific words.

Without conscious effort, Tina began thinking about Tom. She felt good being with him, but things were happening so quickly, she just couldn't be sure if it were — were what? Right? Was that the word she needed?

HER COFFEE CUP was empty, and the clock had moved around to just before nine o'clock. It was time to call the school. Earlier in the week, her student teaching advisor had contacted Tina and given her the name of the woman who would supervise her during the next semester. Mrs. Russell was a true master teacher. Tina had not met her yet, but she knew the woman on sight and by reputation from having observed in the school the year before.

"You'll like her, Tina," Dr. Loren promised. "She'll give you plenty of freedom in class. Some of the master teachers have a difficult time letting a student take over."

"What should I do now?" Tina asked.

"Give her a call next week, just to introduce yourself. She'll be at the school for in-service work and preparing the classroom."

The school secretary told Tina to call Thursday about nine o'clock.

Here goes nothing, she thought, dialing the number. Quickly, the secretary transferred her call. Tina introduced herself to Mrs. Russell, and they began to talk.

"Glad to meet you, Tina. I'm looking forward to working with you this semester."

"Thanks, Mrs. Russell."

"Jayne, please."

"You're kidding!" Tina said aloud before she could stop herself, having put the two names together.

"No," she was told, by a laughing Jayne Russell, "I married into it, so my parents aren't to blame."

"Good," Tina said, laughing along with her. "Is there anything you want me to do in advance?"

"Not really. I'll introduce you to the class on Monday, but the opening unit is a standard one that I use every year. I'll do most of the teaching and just let you get to know the kids. You'll start taking over in the third week, so you'll have plenty of time to get ready. I'll give you all the materials you'll need on Monday. Any questions?"

"No, I don't think so."

"Nervous?"

"Very nervous. You've no idea."

"Sure I do. It never changes. Every year I wonder what the class will be like — fast or slow, easy going or full of trouble makers? It always seems to work out, though. You'll do just fine."

"I hope so."

"You've got Dr. Loren on your side. He raves about you."

"That's good to hear. He's a nice man."

"Good enough. I'll see you next week, then?"

"Yes, thanks. I'm looking forward to it."

"Come in early, if you like. We start at eight, but I'm always here by seven. It might help to just walk around the room a little."

"Okay, thanks. I will."

They said goodby, and that was it until Monday. Tina put the phone back on its cradle but left her hand there for a minute. Jayne Russell? Funny. All the paperwork said Mrs. Russell, without a first name. She sounded really nice, and obviously had a good sense of humor, but even that didn't help Tina with her nerves.

AFTER THE BREAKFAST MEETING, Tom walked out with Masback and a Professor Kniep, trying to figure out just why Masback had wanted him there. The meeting was routine stuff, just committee shuffling and reassignments over waffles and eggs.

"Nice meeting you, Tom," Kniep said, putting out his hand for Tom to shake.

"My pleasure, professor."

"Any more tricks up your sleeve, Aaron?" Kniep asked, turning back to Masback.

"Not right now, Bob," he responded with a big grin.

"What was that all about?" Tom asked, after Professor Kniep had walked off toward the English offices.

"I asked you here when I learned that Bob wouldn't be around to hear your presentation this afternoon. He sits on a university-wide committee that meets at the same time. I just wanted to make sure he had a chance to talk with you, face to face."

"I see," Tom said, still a little curious.

"Every vote counts, Tom. I think you're the best candidate, but you never know. Sorry if it inconvenienced you in any way?"

"No. No problem at all."

"Well, I've got to run now, but I'll see you before your presentation. You've got the room number and all?"

"Yes, thanks."

Just like that, Masback was gone, leaving Tom to wonder if his presence had really been necessary. He had a little over an hour to kill before he would deliver his paper. He found a directory inside one of the pay phones at the cafeteria, but realized that he did not know Tina's last name, nor did he even remember the name of the street she lived on, just that it was two blocks down from his rental. Had they ever exchanged last names? he wondered. Actually, the thought pleased him in a strange way. Just plain Tina and Tom, with no last names, no histories, and no baggage of the past to carry around with them into a new relationship. Romantic as that sounded, however, it did him little good in trying to reach her now. Oh, well, he thought, we'll just have to make do.

Tom stayed in the cafeteria, choosing to people-watch for a while, over a cup of coffee. It was not particularly busy, not like he knew it would be once classes were in session. Registration was going on this week, so the full food services were not yet in operation, and most of the students were outside, standing in one line or another. The faculty meeting had been specially catered in a private back room. The only food available to the public was that in the vending machines lined up on the far wall. Most of the students seated around him were frantically working on their class schedules. Idly, Tom wondered how he would get into the classes he needed, if and when he received the offer.

"Hi, Tom. This is a pleasant surprise."

He looked up to find Tina's friend, the red-headed Maggie, smiling down at him.

"Hi, Maggie," he said, starting to rise.

"Oh, sit down, Tom," she said. "You don't need manners around this place." To prove it, she flopped a schedule of classes onto the table and sat down opposite him. "So, what are you doing here?"

"I'm being interviewed for a teaching position in the English department."

"Very nice. I didn't know you were a professor."

"I'm not. Not yet, anyway. Just getting started, really. It would be a combination teaching job and a fellowship to begin my own doctoral work."

"Well, I hope you get it. Most of the teachers here are ancient."

"Thanks — I think."

"Oh, it was a compliment all right," she said.

Maggie moved both her hands up and behind her head to adjust the simple pony tail she was wearing. She tilted her head down while she was tucking in loose strands of hair, but continued to look at him. The effect of the new angle was somehow erotic, as if she were staring at him from under her long, dark eyelashes, secretive but not coy. No, he thought, Maggie was anything but coy.

"Are you a senior, too?" he asked.

"Uh huh. Me and Tina."

"Maggie," he asked, out of a sudden inspiration, "do you have Tina's number?"

"Sure, at home. Why? Don't you have it? And would you really expect me to give it to you, after I just gave you mine yesterday?" she asked with a smile.

Tom assumed she was just teasing him about the phone number, but he couldn't tell for sure. She might even be upset for all he could read behind that ambiguous smile. For a moment, he was tempted to ask Maggie to call Tina for him when she got home, but he didn't dare.

"So what is going on with you two?" she asked.

"What do you mean?" he said, to gain time, really, having been surprised by her directness.

"You know exactly what I mean," she responded. "Do you have something going with Tina or not?"

"It's a little too early to tell."

"Fair enough," she said. "Some of us like to move a little quicker than others, I suppose."

Maggie deliberately stretched then, without even a pretense of a yawn, the pose raising and elevating her breasts. Tom tried not to look, but couldn't help himself.

When he glanced back up, into her eyes, she was smiling at him, openly, confidently.

"The year's young," she said, picking up her schedule of classes. "And it looks like we'll both be here for a while. See you around campus."

Tom watched as she stood and moved off across the cafeteria. No, he thought again, there's nothing coy or subtle about Maggie. After she left, Tom realized he could have asked Maggie for Tina's last name, had he not gotten distracted. But that would have sounded just as silly as asking for her phone number. Once again, Tom wondered just how good a friend Maggie was to Tina. With friends like that, you would really have to watch your back. There I go being judgmental again, he warned himself, stifling the reaction. Maggie might be a fine-looking woman, but he did not trust her, not one little bit.

TINA WAITED AT HOME until eleven o'clock that morning, pretending to read in one of the library books. Actually the book was quite good, but she couldn't concentrate. The phone rang twice, but there was no response to her hello, even though she could tell someone was there, listening. Each time, Tina hoped it was Tom. Each time there was only silence.

The hands of the clock were dragging. She grew more and more irritated. What should she do? she asked herself. Sit around here, all day, waiting for him? Supposedly, he was up every day at five or six o'clock, running on the beach, yet today he could not find the time to contact her. Not even a phone call. What was she, some kind of satellite to his whim, dependent on his movements for her sense of meaning? She imagined a moon spinning around an earth, both spinning around a sun, but that picture made her think of Aunt Aimee. Now that would really do it. The last thing Tina needed was someone who could look into a crystal ball and see her future.

The phone rang again. "Hello," she said, after picking it up quickly, expecting it to be Tom finally calling, but instead it was Anna asking about the beach. "Yes, I may come down later," Tina told her. "Okay."

After hanging up the phone, Tina went back to thinking about her aunt again. Aimee was once a devout and orthodox Catholic, but now she was into the world of horoscopes and astrology, all the while insisting that the occult was not in violation of Church teaching, in fact, it was an art older than Christianity. Maybe Aunt Aimee could read the stars and tell me what to do, she thought. Tina could even remember some of the terms her aunt used. One was the conjunction of planets in one house of the zodiac. She and Tom had been here, together, in this house, her house. Were they like two planets moving closer and closer together? Or was Tom just a comet roaring through her life? Why did he have the power to irritate her so?

Tina opened the book and tried again to read. Once more the phone rang without anyone being there, at least anyone who would speak. That made three times this morning alone. She didn't think Tom would be calling like that and hanging up, but if it weren't Tom calling, who could it be? She hoped it wasn't another crank like she'd had two years earlier. Calls all day and night without a voice, just a hangup, until she finally had the number changed.

The next time she looked at the clock, it was almost high noon. Carefully, she placed the book on the coffee table, noticing, even as she did it, that she lined up the sides and corners of the book with the sides and corners of the table. She felt sad and disappointed, but she wasn't going to let Tom ruin her day. Why were men like this? she wondered. They make all these promises, only to let you down. This is ridiculous, she thought, gathering up her stuff for the beach. If Tom really wanted to see her, then he could just try to find her. Off she stomped, feeling ridiculous even as she did it, but unable to stop. Before she reached the corner, she was walking normally again, having put the childishness behind her.

The two-block walk to the beach felt good, just getting out of the house and exercising. Why did women feel they needed a man to be complete? True love? Go where I go, do as I do? But that was the Ruth and Naomi story, about two women, a story which reminded her of her mother. Deliberately, trying not to think about Tom, she made the mistake of thinking about her mother, which led her right back to the evening before, full circle back to Tom's absence, her reason for being with her mother, in the first place. Damn! Her mother had even asked about Ted.

"His name is Ed, Mother."

"Oh, yes, Ed."

Her mother had met Ed just once, but she never could seem to get his name right, no matter how simple it was.

"How is he?" she asked. "How are you getting along?"

Her mother had broken out in a big smile when Tina finally mentioned having met a new guy, a knowing, adult, motherly, and absolutely nauseating smile, so much as to say, Now we are getting somewhere! Good grief, Tina had only wanted to talk, not bring Tom home to dinner or to get engaged. As usual, her mother had been no help, other than being her usual distracted self, supportive, but part of another generation. It had been a mistake going last night. Why do I keep going back, trying to please her? Tina wondered. The only thing that would really please her mother would be a grandchild. Once again, she mentioned how many of her friends' daughters were pregnant. Hint, hint!

What do I want? Tina asked herself. *Really? What do I want for myself, not for my mother?* How about just getting through my senior year and the student teaching, with no complications? How would that be? Once again she was irritated. First at Tom, then at her mother. Just wait till I see him again! But would she see him again?

Four hours later, as Tina sat on the beach, she still did not know the answer, and she was more irritated than ever, especially after spending time with the old gang, dodging their leading questions about her new friend.

"Is anything happening there?"

"Any prospects?"

"Who is he?" Judy asked, not having met Tom the day before. "What's his name?"

"Tom."

"Where is he today?" Maggie wanted to know as she stretched out on her towel. She had just come down to the beach after being on campus for registration. "Is he still in town?"

"Yes, he's still here."

"Are you going to see him later?" Maggie asked.

"Oh, probably," Tina replied.

Tina tried to sound certain, though she was beginning to wonder herself. Maggie's questions were strangely pointed and prying, innocent on the surface, but with some other agenda underneath. And why should Maggie be so interested in the first place? Other than the usual reason that Maggie was interested in all men.

After a few minutes, the conversation moved on to something else, giving Tina chance to relax. They didn't mean any real harm, she thought, just teasing and being naturally curious. Most of her friends were seniors, too. There was an unstated feeling that you had to be engaged, or at least pinned, by your senior year. Otherwise, your life would be dull, empty and meaningless. Some of her unattached friends were actually starting to panic.

Tina's girlfriends on the beach finally stopped grilling her when they realized she did not want to talk about Tom or their relationship. Ed was nowhere to be seen, but Tina had the feeling that he had been there, spotted her, and gone in the other direction. Men! Who could understand them?

TOM SAT IN THE FRONT ROW while Dr. Masback introduced him to the assembled faculty and students. How many were there? Twenty or thirty? There seemed to be more faculty than students. He was to talk for twenty minutes on a subject of his choice, with a question-and-answer period to follow.

"— he holds a master's degree in English and will be talking about allegory in the modern American novel."

Tom prepared himself to rise, but Masback continued on, telling the group how they had met. Tom only half-listened, having heard him tell the story before, and returned to his previous train of thought. He'd had an hour to look over his notes, to get himself prepared. Tom spent the time sitting under a huge tree in the campus quad area. He thought about presenting one of several papers he had written in the past, having brought two of them with him to

Golden Shore, but they were regurgitations of other people's theories. As he inspected the huge tree, Tom knew that his first idea would be more dangerous but more challenging, and potentially far more rewarding.

His training was in Renaissance literature, but his particular interest was in allegory, a literary mode that many supposedly knowledgeable people thought had died out in the middle ages. Allegory was alive and well, of course, having just shifted form and focus. Tom was not alone in believing this, but he thought that he had some interesting things to add about certain contemporary authors, Thomas Pynchon for one. Once again, Tom glanced at his notes, sensing that Masback was just about to finish up.

"— it is my pleasure to welcome him here, today. Tom?" the professor said, motioning for him to come up to the podium, as a scattered round of applause began.

Tom took a slow, deep breath, stood, and walked toward the front of the room, as well-prepared as he could be for this moment. He would be launching himself into areas of conjecture, into unfamiliar territory. Why not discover in his first at bat whether or not he belonged here? Tom liked the baseball image, now that he had applied it. Yes, he would ignore the bunt sign and go for the home run. Nothing ventured, nothing gained.

AS SHE PARKED, Tina could hear the sounds of the children at play from the other side of the building. All summer long, she had worked here, at the university's preschool and summer experimental program for grade school ages. The pay was not particularly good, but she jumped at the chance to get some practical experience before beginning her student teaching. She loved it, every single minute. She made mistakes. She learned. She grew. Most importantly, Tina got to experience teaching, learning that it was right for her. Every day she went home content. The job officially ended last Friday, but the director asked her to come by today, at this time, for an exit interview and to pick up her final check. The money would come in handy for her upcoming book expenses. As she walked up the steps, she thought again of Tom, wondering how he could just disappear like that, without a trace? She had waited for him on the beach, as long as she could, but he never came, and there had been no note on her door at home. Maybe she was making too much out of the past few days, but she really thought they were doing well together. She opened the front door to the school and walked in.

"Surprise!"

They were all there. Children, teachers, some of the parents. The kids had made a sign that stretched across the back wall: TO OUR FAVORITE INTURN. Tina had to laugh at the spelling. They'd obviously done the sign on their own. One of her favorite pupils ran up and hugged her around the legs. Her name was Olivia. A bright child but learning-disabled, with very special needs. She'd been a challenge for Tina.

"Tina, Tina. Come see what I've done."

"In a minute, Olivia. I promise."

Tina had worked with her all summer, an hour or two a day, teaching her alternative ways of studying, ways that would capitalize on her strengths instead of expose her weaknesses. Slow going at first, but when the child finally got the idea, she took off at breakneck speed, smiling all the way. The program director walked up and put an arm around Tina's shoulders, not wanting to disturb the children gathered around below.

"Did we surprise you?" she asked, grinning.

"You sure did," Tina said, through her tears. "Thanks."

WHEN TOM FINISHED with the last of the questions, he was drained but contented. Contented was a funny word for what he felt, but it fit. He wasn't sure yet how to evaluate the experience. His talk had gone all right, as well as could be expected on such an impromptu basis. It would have been smoother had he been given more time to prepare. He used notes he had developed under the tree for about the first half, but then he found himself launching off into a whole new forest of ideas. Tom had taken a chance on something experimental, something that interested him. He stumbled twice, having to think on his feet when he reached some thorny places in his logic, but managed to extricate himself. All in all, he was satisfied.

During the question-and-answer period, he fielded the first two or three queries easily. The questions were obvious and so were his answers. Then Tom had been metaphorically nailed to the tree. A professor in the third row had exposed a major weakness in Tom's argument, one he had not seen, let alone anticipated. Why would a modern novelist use such an archaic form? What could he hope to gain, given a modern audience who were unfamiliar with the mode? Tom could feel the blood pounding in his temples, but his head remained clear.

He asked for further clarification and got it. In turn, he then asked the professor a question. Had Dante written for himself or for a knowledgeable audience? They began a dialogue while the rest of the audience listened. Together,

Tom and the professor moved toward solving the problem. At one point, Tom acknowledged a graduate student in the back whose question helped further their process. Soon, others were joining in a lively discussion that was actually an academic debate. Tom was exhilarated by the experience. He did not have the complete answer to the problem raised, but he was close.

As the hour wound down, Tom looked around the room for a final question to field and saw Dr. Masback in the back row, grinning at him, giving the thumbs-up sign.

TINA FINALLY GOT HOME about five-thirty. The party had been a wonderful experience, making her feel truly valued. The idea of student teaching wasn't nearly as frightening now, as it had been yesterday. After the party, the director hugged Tina and told her that she'd "sail through" her next semester with flying colors. Tina drove home experiencing a high that was only now starting to abate. Two of her girlfriends called, checking on her plans for the evening, offering some ideas. No, thanks, she told them. Tonight, she was going to stay home and rest up, maybe shampoo her hair. She wasn't the least bit hungry after the cake and ice cream of the party, so she just fixed a cup of tea and sat down on the couch to think through the day.

In spite of all the good things that had happened, she couldn't help but be disappointed by Tom's not showing up or calling. Where had he been? He knew where she lived, but now even that knowledge irritated her. Well, it was up to him. Not one single word, all day long! As the evening wore on and the euphoria of the party started to fade, she found herself growing nervous and irritable. Twice more the phone rang without a response, except for a pause and a hang up. Those calls were no help either, as they added to her growing sense of frustration.

Tina thought about getting out of the house for a while, maybe even out of town. Just leave. Get in the car and go somewhere. Drive up the coast to her cousin Suzie's place, perhaps. It was only a hundred miles. She could stay for three or four days and come back just in time for classes to begin.

I might just do it, she thought, but first she needed to get cleaned up, take a bath, shampoo her hair, and then she would do something, she was not sure what, but something. Two hours later, Tina was still lying on the couch, turning the pages of her book. She had tried television, but there was nothing on except for reruns. The rabbit ears didn't pull in a very good picture, anyhow. She was feeling hurt now, not just irritated. On the verge of tears, Tina had to do something. Perhaps she should do the laundry. At least she could get something productive out of the evening.

When the doorbell rang, Tina jumped up, in spite of herself. She was past irritation, past hurt, having moved into a dull, gray neutrality of self-protection. Even though she was tempted to ignore the bell, she was already on her feet. Refusing to answer it would be childish. She might just as well see what Tom had to say for himself. In spite of her irritation, Tina really did want to tell Tom about the party, too. Walking across the room, she thought: How ironic! Here I am, an independent, modern woman who does not even have the option of ignoring a man, of refusing to answer the door bell. They knock, we jump. Tina was both too happy and too frustrated not to answer the door. She had too much news to tell him and too many questions to ask. Reaching the door, she opened it, not quite ready for a confrontation, but certainly ready for some answers. But it was not Tom standing there.

"Ed! What are you doing here?" she asked, knowing how silly it sounded even as she said it. Two days ago, he had been her boyfriend, sort of. Ed had been here before, several times. Often.

"Where is he?" Ed demanded.

"Tom's not here," she answered, without having to ask whom Ed meant by *him*.

"Bullshit! I've seen you two together, all over town. The beach, the pier."

Had Ed been following them, the whole time? It would explain the strange feeling she had of being watched.

"He's not here, Ed. I haven't seen him all day."

"I don't believe you. You're sleeping with him, aren't you?" he accused her. When she did not respond, other than to stare at him in shock, he reached out and grabbed her by the shoulders, shaking her. "Tell me the truth!" he demanded.

"Ed! Stop it! Do you hear me? Stop it!"

Tina had never seen him like this before. She could smell the beer on his breath, as he suddenly moved to kiss her. With all her strength, she tried to push him away, but he was far too big and powerful. Violently, he pulled her back, ripping the sleeve of her blouse in the process. They both froze at the sound, looking down at the damage.

"You bitch," he snarled, grabbing both sides of her blouse and tearing it all the way down the front, the buttons flying and ricocheting off the floor.

She stood there, in her bra, the tattered pieces of her blouse hanging at her sides. My God, he's going to rape me, she thought, trying to cover herself.

"Please don't, Ed. Please!" she tried to say, but it came out as a mere whisper.

For a moment they just stood there, Tina trying to cover her nakedness, Ed staring at her, breathing heavily. Then he started to cry. Cry like a baby. Deep, wrenching sobs.

"I'm sorry," he blubbered. "I'm sorry!" He could not stop crying. Looking at her through his tears, he said, "I love you, Tina. I love you."

But when he reached out for her, she screamed and jumped back. It was not a loud scream but a scream nonetheless. His whole being seemed to go limp as he stood there, staring at her for what seemed like minutes but was probably just seconds. Without another word, he turned and walked out of the house and into the night, shaking his head as he went.

Tina stood there for a moment, still in shock. Then slowly she moved to the door, closed and locked it. Making her way to the couch, she sat down, and then she was crying. In pain, in fear, in relief, in anger. She had gone from a party to this? What was happening to her life?

"HAVE YOU EVER THOUGHT of the relationship between James Joyce and Pynchon?" Tom was asked. Before he could answer, someone else whom Tom had not met, yet, joined the conversation.

"Yes, I think Joyce would be fruitful because of *Ulysses,*" the woman was saying, "because of what he did with the older patterns of the *Odyssey,* bringing them into a modern world."

Tom was happy to be let off the hook for a minute as the other two continued the conversation without needing his feedback. He and The Committee were walking to the faculty dining room, where he would be — he had almost thought "wined and dined," but there would be no wine for him. Tom would meet more of the department faculty and some of the specially-invited students majoring in English, a few of whom would be in the classes he might be teaching. Slow down! he warned himself. You did well enough, but the offer has not been made, not yet. Still, he couldn't help but be optimistic. Masback seemed certain that Tom was the leading candidate, but he was Tom's mentor, so who knew for sure? As the group began filing into the faculty building, Tom thought of Tina again, wishing that she were with him, right now. Soon enough, he thought, soon enough.

The evening session was to be something more casual. A social event, really, Masback had said. Again, Tom wished he had Tina's phone number, so he could at least check in with her, letting her know what was going on. Funny that she would be the first person he thought of when the grilling ended. Funny but nice. He could hardly wait to tell her how things had gone. Tom had more thinking to do, more analyzing, but he was beginning to believe that this might really be possible. He was starting to feel confident enough that he belonged in this atmosphere, that he could actually pull this thing off, earn the degree, teach, and maybe even become a writer. He felt full of hope.

TINA TOOK A LONG SHOWER, trying to wash the experience away. Lots of soap. Lots of water. Afterwards, she grew suddenly tired, too tired to eat, though she tried, too tired even to make it into bed. She collapsed on the sofa and was asleep in an instant. Some time later, she awakened to a gentle knocking on the door. This time she knew it was Tom because his knock was some kind of a code that she recognized from the morning before, like "Shave and a haircut, six bits." She did not want him to see her like this, but she had to let him in — no idea why, other than instinct and the need for human contact. She opened the door and fell into his arms, so tired she could hardly hold herself up.

"My God, what's wrong?" he asked. "What happened?" Tom helped her back to the couch, almost carrying her. Then she was in his arms, sobbing, hanging on for her life. They stayed like that, with arms around each other, for a long time, until she was through crying. Continuing to hold her, he said, very gently, "Tell me about it."

Surprising herself, she did. She told him everything. "All week, I had the strangest feeling of being followed. It was Ed. He admitted it — I think he's been calling here and hanging up, too — I couldn't help it, but I was so angry at you for not calling or coming by — and he tore my blouse — he'd been drinking — I could smell it on him — I was terrified he was going to rape me — but when he left, I just collapsed on the couch." Everything got said, all of it, the words spilling out like a waterfall, purifying. She knew the story was disjoint, the words making little sense, even as she said them, but it felt so good telling him, getting it out, releasing it all.

"Ed's the big guy, right?" he asked.

"Yes, he's a football player," she answered, before she had fully assimilated his tone.

"I will kill the son of a bitch," he said.

She heard the words — absolutely flat, apparently devoid of emotion. No obvious anger. Not even frustration.

Just the cold promise of the grave. She knew he meant it. If Ed were here now, Tom would kill him, without hesitation, in the blink of an eye.

"No, Tom." Now she was comforting him, holding him to herself, as best she could, because he sat there, stone rigid. Slowly, carefully, she knew that she had to explain it all again. This time, without tears. This time, you mustn't cry, she told herself.

"Ed didn't rape me, Tom — really, he didn't even touch me or hurt me. Not much, anyway. Just the blouse. I don't even think that was deliberate. I was more afraid than anything else, shocked really." Tina looked at Tom, but his expression hadn't changed, not yet. She continued, watching him as she spoke, "I even feel sorry for him, in a way. He cried, like a baby, so I know he was sorry." She started to tell Tom that Ed had said he loved her, but she thought better of it. "He never wanted to hurt me," Tina said, "not intentionally."

"You're really all right?" Tom finally asked, after a long pause, appearing to be completely calm. But he had been calm when she held him, before. Too calm, frighteningly calm.

"Yes, I'm fine. Honestly."

He looked into her eyes, deeply, before nodding. Moving mechanically, he fixed her a sandwich and a cup of tea. They continued talking while she ate. In answer to her question, Tom apologized for not being able to get in touch with her, explaining that he had gotten a call from the university early that morning.

"They wanted me on campus right away. There wasn't enough time to let you know," he said, looking at her, a look that asked her to understand, to forgive him. "I didn't have your telephone number, or I would have called."

He was apologizing for not being here, with her, taking the blame on himself. It was all his fault somehow. He actually believed it. Tina could see it in his eyes, hear it in his words.

"Tom, there was nothing you could have done about any of this. It isn't your fault, it isn't my fault. In a weird way, it isn't even Ed's fault." Tom continued to look at her, blankly, but she felt that he was relaxing a little bit, easing off. Maybe she could get him to talk? "What happened on campus?" she asked.

"I was there the whole day," he responded, his voice flat, pausing to add, again, "there was no time to let you know." But after a few seconds, he did continue, "The session yesterday was an interview by the full committee. I did all right because it was all about background, training, my own interests. This morning's session was a breakfast really, just a committee meeting, but I got to meet more of the department. In the afternoon session, they asked me to deliver an impromptu lecture and then grilled me all over again, afterwards. In the evening, I got to meet the whole department, but I didn't have to do anything. It was just a social event, a dinner to kick off the new school year."

Tom seemed to be finished for a while, so she changed the subject and told him about the party, how she had been surprised and delighted. How good it made her feel.

"A lot of the parents came, too, the first time I got to meet many of them," she told him. "It was good, getting to match the kids up with their moms and dads."

Tom was watching her, tracking the conversation, but he still seemed to be distracted, his mind elsewhere, in dangerous, violent places, Tina suspected. Instinctively, she again changed the subject, moving it back to him.

"Tell me how your lecture went," she asked, trying to imagine him in front of an audience.

At first he responded in a monotone, but gradually, slowly, he warmed up to the story. "It went all right. I talked on allegory and the modern novel — hidden meanings, religious interpretations. Actually, the whole thing was energizing, and I walked away with several good ideas. New ideas. Maybe I'm fooling myself, but the farther away from it that I get, the better it seems. By tomorrow, I'll probably be a genius — in my own mind, anyway," he said, even managing to smile, after glancing at Tina, including her in the joke.

"Did you get all the information on pay and benefits?" she asked. "You were wondering about that yesterday."

"Yes," he responded, "it looks pretty good."

"Tell me about it. What did you decide?" she asked.

As Tom explained the options, the finances and health package, Tina grew very tired, so tired she couldn't hold up her head. She tried to listen, wanting more than anything to know if he had taken the offer.

She woke to feel herself being carried, gently cradled in his arms. Tom sat her on the edge of the bed, folded back the covers, and then tucked her in, robe and all. Tina watched him with wonder, almost detached from the scene in which she was a part. How could this man whisper the promise of death, one moment, and then be so gentle, the next?

"Sleep now," he said. "I'll be on the couch if you need me. See you in the morning."

He reached down, gently touching her on the forehead and the cheek, and then he bent down to kiss her softly on the lips. She fell asleep so quickly, she could still feel the pressure of his kiss on her mouth.

TINA AWOKE with a start, the sound of his shouting still in her ears. A horrible sound, mostly like a scream, but worse. Like something she had seen or heard in a movie once. Perhaps the final, blood stroke of a gladiator or the howling of an animal. Quickly she went to the doorway of the front room. She could see him on the couch, struggling in his sleep. The light coming from the street showed her that his eyes were closed, that he really was asleep, dreaming. But this was more than a dream. It was a full-blown nightmare. She looked at the clock across the room. Middle of the night. Tina watched for a long time, until she was certain that he was sleeping peacefully, again. Who was this man? Where had he been? And where were they headed? She found herself praying as she stood there in the hall. No matter what else, Tina believed in God and trusted that He was in ultimate control of this world. Before returning to bed, she sent up one last petition — God, help us, please!

Chapter Five: Friday

SHE WOKE BEFORE HE DID, surprising them both. Tina felt shy and awkward, at first, until she realized that Tom did, too. They were quiet and careful with each other as they ate the breakfast she prepared. Solicitous was the right term, she thought. As if the wrong word could break the other, like a heavy knife on an egg shell. Tina sensed that they had moved into a new stage in their relationship. The kiss had been part of it. That and holding each other. They had even slept together — separately, to be sure — but in the same house. Tina knew that she had revealed more to Tom than she ever planned or expected. She guessed that he was probably feeling the same way. All the events of the night before were facts. They had happened, nothing could change that, but how those facts would change her or them and their relationship, Tina did not know. All that was yet to be determined.

"Thanks, Tom," she ventured.

"For what? I didn't do anything. I only wish I'd been here. To stop it."

"You were here, when I needed you."

"Still, I just wish —" he started to say.

"You helped," Tina interrupted him. "Just by staying with me last night, you helped."

She wasn't sure whether Tom believed her or not, but she had said the important stuff. It was enough for now.

After breakfast, Tom went back to his apartment to change and clean up. With him gone, Tina ran around her house, picking up, doing what little cleaning she thought necessary. She knew it was silly. After all, if anything were messy, he'd already seen it. But she still wanted the place to look nice. It was her home. She thought of running down to the highway for some flowers, but didn't want to take the chance of missing his return. One last look around, then off she went to comb her hair and dress for the day.

Surprising herself, Tina suddenly realized that she was feeling happy, expectant, and eager to get on with life, whatever wonderful things it might hold. How had she gone from the events of last night to the mood of today? In a psychology class, they had studied manic depression. Was this some kind of manic reaction after the events of yesterday? It made no sense on a rational level, but maybe, just maybe, she could leave all the thinking behind for a day. Feeling the need for music, she spun the dial until she found a station that matched her mood. Upbeat rock with happy lyrics. Nothing sad would do. For a second, she hesitated, warning herself not to fly off too fast into unknown spaces. Nice and easy does it. But those were also song lyrics. "Nice and easy does it all the time," she sung within her mind. Eddie Arnold, she thought. But that song was too slow and too hesitant for her. She ignored her own warning and soon found herself humming in front of her vanity. She smiled into the mirror, liking what she saw.

AFTER HIS SHOWER, Tom decided to call Wayne, his AA sponsor. He had promised to let Wayne know how the interview went at school, so he dialed the number of his sponsor's office.

"Hi, Wayne. It's Tom."

"Hey, how did everything go?"

Tom went through all the highlights of the past two days. How he enjoyed the experience, liked the school. The department looked good. The faculty he met were encouraging. His presentation went well.

"Did you get to a meeting?" Wayne asked, meaning an AA meeting.

"Yes. It was all right." Tom described the meeting he had attended, the nature of the group. What he had liked and what he had not. Wayne asked if he had stuck out his hand, tried to meet some new people? Tom said yes, he had, and then described the ending of the meeting, when he had stood in the prayer circle, holding hands with a seventy-year-old Mexican named Julian and an eighteen-year-old student named Brian who was going to have a birthday the next week. He named a couple of other people and then started winding down the conversation, not wanting to keep Wayne too long on his business number.

"Oh, yes," Tom said, adding it almost as an afterthought. "I met a woman on the beach."

"Oh, you did, did you?" said Wayne, suddenly interested anew. "Tell me about her."

Conscious of how long they had already talked, Tom did not go into the events of the night before. He just described Tina, told Wayne what he knew about her, how they seemed to be getting along pretty well. Finishing up, Tom asked what his friend thought.

"She sounds nice. Just take it easy. Nice and easy. One day at a time. You've got a lot going on right now. Give me a call tomorrow. I've got to go now. The other line is ringing. Bye."

Now that the call was over, Tom realized he really wanted to talk some more with his friend about Tina. It may have been the main reason he called in the first place. Was it okay to get into a relationship? Should he tell Tina about his being an alcoholic? Should he wait? Tom had a pretty good idea what Wayne would say to that question. Why haven't you told her already? What are you waiting for? A good question, what was he waiting for?

LATER, TINA TOOK TOM to one of her favorite places in The Shore, feeling pleased to show it to him. They spent the morning walking the beach on the ocean side, away from the bay, poking through the tide pools, looking at the sea creatures there, starfish and urchins. The wonders of God's world, she thought to herself. Above them flocks of sea gulls squawked their complaints, the braver ones walking and hopping along the sand to beg a meal.

"Look, Tom," Tina hollered, pointing to the sea, thinking she had seen a pilot whale off shore, but it could have been a porpoise or a seal, although it looked bigger.

"Where?" he asked, trying to follow the direction she was indicating. By the time that Tom looked, the creature was back under, whatever it was.

"I think it was a whale."

"Really? A big one."

"No," she answered, "just a pilot whale. We get them every so often. Sometimes in groups."

"This is really nice," Tom said, after giving up on finding the whale. "For the first time this week, I really, truly feel like I'm on vacation."

"I'm glad," she answered.

They did not talk much for a while. Tina thought it was a good day for adventure, a day of abundance. She knew it was a good day for healing. She already felt better.

A COUPLE OF TIMES, Tom was tempted to talk seriously about their relationship, but he held off. What could he say that wouldn't ruin the mood and spirit of the day? He was getting to see a different side of Tina. That was good enough. And for the first time that week, Tom truly felt like he was on holiday, on a vacation. He thoroughly enjoyed the day, a day of fun and games, just playing in the sun. No big deals. He needed a day like this. Wayne had been right. He had a lot going on right now. For just this one day, Tom wanted to play. It felt very good. It had been a long, long time.

On a whim, he dipped a finger in the water and sprayed Tina as she leaned over a pool of urchins. The act was done even before he had time to stop himself. If he had thought about it, first, he might not have done it.

"I'm sorry," he apologized. "I just couldn't resist." Seeing the shocked look on her face, he couldn't help but laugh. "You look so funny."

"Oh, you're going to get it now," she said, pushing the sun hat back off her face, as she filled both hands with water before dousing him.

"Okay, you asked for it!" he answered back, feeling himself break into a grin.

Soon they were throwing water at each other, then sand, and even pieces of seaweed. When Tina tried to dodge away, he stalked her. Back-and-forth she went, trying to elude him, laughing happily the whole time.

"No, you don't," he cried.

"Yes, I do," she responded, giggling.

Her laughter pleased Tom, pleased him very much. She needs a day like this, too, he thought. Finally, she bolted, taking off across the sand. Tom gave her a decent head start, admiring the way she moved, the graceful way she ran, then took off after her.

"Help, help," she screamed in mock terror, looking back at his pursuit.

Finally, trying to dodge to the right, she slipped and fell to the sand, scrambling to get back up, but laughing too hard to make it. Laughing with her and at her, Tom slid to the sand beside her.

"Gotcha!" he said. "Do you yield?"

"Never!"

"Say uncle," he demanded, tickling her side.

"Oh, no. Please don't. I'm ticklish."

That was all Tom needed to hear. He continued tickling her until she was laughing, crying and squirming, all at once. "Do you give up?" he asked.

"Yes, yes. Anything. Just stop."

"A kiss, then. For a boon?"

Tom continued to stare into her eyes, until she could stop laughing and return his look. Very slowly and gently, he kissed her. When she did not shy away but searched his eyes in response, he kissed her again.

THESE WERE DIFFERENT, Tina thought. Yes, these were real kisses. Last night had been something else, altogether. What had that other kiss meant? Good night? I'm sorry it happened? Something like that, she supposed. As she lay on her back, holding his hand, she knew these new kisses had been special. The first was like a game, a token she had to pay, but the second was serious, the I-care-for-you, do-you-care-for-me variety. She responded because the kiss was so gentle. Even before she could start to be afraid, he took her hand and stretched out on the sand next to her.

Thank you, Tom, she thought to herself, feeling the strength in his hand. Thanks for understanding. Tina wasn't sure if he were awake or asleep. She even wondered if she had fallen asleep for a little while? Why not? The morning drifted away in a collage of pleasant memories. It was a good day. One of the best.

TOM AWAKENED, slowly and carefully searching his mind for a dream. He looked in every corner, but there had been none. Anytime he could sleep without dreaming was a bonus. He was on a beach, lying in the warm sand, but this was not Vietnam. In his own hand, he felt the smaller fingers of a woman's hand, warm and soft. Tom turned his head to that side. On the sand next to him lay Tina, breathing easily. He looked at her, but she was either asleep, herself, or being very quiet behind closed eyes.

How had this happened, when he was least expecting it? *My God*, he thought, *how can I handle a relationship, now, with everything up in the air?* Tom knew that his recovery was solid, but that he couldn't afford to get complacent about it. He had only been sober a year, not even that long, yet. Now he might even be changing jobs, moving to a brand new area. He was excited about the possibilities, but wary, at the same time. Tom had seen and heard too many horror stories about stress causing a relapse into drinking, even after many years of sobriety. Staying sober had to be his number one priority. Without sobriety he had nothing. Nothing at all.

Tom felt himself drawing back inside a safety zone. Easy does it, he told himself, easy does it.

AS THEY RETURNED to her place for lunch, Tina thought Tom was a little reserved. Maybe he's just sluggish after their nap? She could relate to that. Sleeping during the day threw her off-schedule, too. Once back inside her house, Tom saw a block of photographs on the kitchen counter. They were pictures of her, a professional set she'd just had taken.

"What are these?" he asked.

"My senior pictures," she replied. "We can submit our own prints instead of using the school service. I sat for those a couple of weeks ago."

After lunch, while they were having a cup of coffee, he went to the counter and brought the pictures back. "May I have one of them?" he asked. "I've got an idea for it."

"Sure," she responded, pleased that he would want one.

"Let's go to my place for a minute." Curious, she agreed. She finished the dishes while he carefully cut one of the pictures from the page, after which he started making some ink sketches on typing paper he borrowed from her. *What is he up to?* she wondered.

"NOW WHERE DID I PUT that stuff?" Tom mumbled to himself, impatient to get started.

"I didn't know you were an artist," she said.

Tom was moving about the main room of his apartment, gathering together a box of chalk sticks and a pad of clean white paper, quality art paper. He went back to the drawer of the dresser and returned with some charcoal pencils.

"I'm not, really. This is therapy."

"What do you mean therapy?" she asked.

Images of the VA hospital flashed through his mind, coupled with scenes from Vietnam, often the subject of his art work while a patient. "Just a manner of speaking," he said, changing the subject and trying to change the memories. "Art is supposed to free the inner soul, or so someone told me once. There, now I've got it all together."

Tom had no illusions about his talent. He could work up a portrait or a seascape, but only when he had a photograph to copy, a fixed and frozen model on paper, one that did not move or change colors before his eyes. He had known real artists, had seen them at work, daring nature, challenging her changing face, but he had no such abilities. He was just a craftsman, a draftsman.

"What I'm going to do now is use the photograph to get the major outlines for the portrait and go from there."

"Like a paint-by-numbers set?" she asked.

"I guess so," he answered, looking at her to see if she were teasing him. She was. Her smile gave it away. "A little more sophisticated, I suppose, but not by much," he smiled in return.

Yes, working from the photograph, he exactly copied the major outlines of the figure, often using a ruler to do it, carefully and precisely filling in the details. He would not even need Tina here, in order to work up the sketch. But he wanted her here, sitting by the window, in the same pose as the photo. He liked her company. Tom felt himself going a little flat after their busy day and the success of the day before. Self-doubt was creeping back in. When would the university call? Would he get the offer or not? Working on the portrait would help him pass the time, peacefully.

"Should I do anything special?" she asked. "I mean do I have to freeze?"

"Just look beautiful," he answered, glancing at her, with a smile. "That should be easy enough."

He did look at her, periodically, as he drew with the charcoal, but it was the photograph that fixed her image. She could not hold still, not completely. No model could, and the light changed all the time, even as he worked. *No*, he thought, *I'm a technician, not an artist.*

TINA LIKED WATCHING him work. It pleased her to be his subject. She was usually camera shy, embarrassed by the picture-taking process, until the photographer could get her to relax. The better ones could, not by telling her she was pretty because that did not work, but by joking, easing the tension. Was she pretty? She had heard it all her life, but knew that she did not believe it, not completely, then or now. Tom had just said she was beautiful, kidding, but it pleased her, anyway. It pleased her very much. Maybe he was merely being polite? She hoped not.

Compliments bothered her and always had, for as long back as she could remember. Somehow it all went back to her parents' divorce. Why? She did not know, not completely. She partly understood, mostly from education classes, that her self-confidence had been shattered, way back when, and had never been fully restored. Theories and words. As a child, she believed the divorce had been her fault. A portion of her still believed it now. If only she had not asked her mother about the lady her daddy was kissing. If only she had just gotten her drink of water and gone back to bed.

"Can I get up and move for a minute?" she asked, feeling antsy. Tom had been working steadily for a long time now but looked as if he would have continued, driven on, had she not spoken.

"Sure, let's take a break. My back could use the rest," he said, flexing.

"Can I see it?" she asked, feeling curious but shy.

"No. It's very bad luck," he teased her, closing the pad with a smile.

Tina was disappointed but chalked his refusal up to artistic temperament. She would get to see it later on.

They decided to walk down to the cafe on the pier for a snack, just malts and fries, because he had nothing fit to eat. There were two cans of chili and a box of cereal in the cupboard. His refrigerator contained half-a-quart of milk, two cans of Pepsi, and something in a carry out box.

"How long has this been here?" she asked.

"Let's see," he answered, "Not more than three days."

"No fungus, yet?" she joked, but he had already gone back to working on the portrait, even though they had just decided to leave.

For a minute, she looked around the apartment, again. She had already studied it, earlier, while he was working. Tom was meticulously neat about some things. The room was picked up, with no clothes lying about on the floor or on the backs of chairs, but there were two piles of books stacked on the coffee table, with scraps of paper stuck between the pages. When did he find the time to read? Had he brought the books with him, or were they from the university library? Were they texts that he would be using to teach from in a week? She wanted to ask if he had gotten the offer and decided to take it, but she held back, irrationally afraid that he had not. She was certain that Tom would tell her when he found out, or when he decided. Wouldn't he?

"Are you ready to go, Tom?" she asked, knowing it would interrupt him but getting hungrier by the minute.

"Sure," he said, dropping the pencil before closing the tablet again.

They didn't talk much during the walk. Tom seemed preoccupied. Perhaps with the portrait? she wondered. A couple of times, she tried to get him to talk about his artwork.

"Do you have any formal training?"

"No, just tinkering around."

"Have you saved some of it?" she asked.

"Good grief, no," he said, looking at her as if shocked, somehow.

Now what was that all about? she wondered. Tom seemed reluctant to talk, so she let the matter drop. Maybe he was just tired. She was getting that way herself. Over the rest of the walk to the pier, she replayed the day, trying to retrieve and relive the pleasant memories of the morning. It had been a great morning, but not every minute of every day can be like that, she told herself. Can it? Quiet times were necessary, too. As they walked in silence the rest of the way, Tina wondered what Tom was thinking about.

I SHOULD HAVE KNOW BETTER, he thought. Artwork never did relax me. He really had started it in the VA hospital, as therapy, but it just pushed all his perfectionism buttons — this is not good enough, it will never be good enough, why did you do that, and what's wrong with this color? Doing scenes from Vietnam had helped him process some of his experiences, but not all, not by a long shot. And now, what he really wanted was a phone call from the university, so he would know one way or another. This limbo of indecision was unbearable.

What kind of company was he being for Tina? he wondered. What was he going to do with her, or about her? Next week, he might be back home and at work. What then? Maybe they should just put everything on hold? Or was it too late for that? He could not stop thinking about the beach this morning. He never should have kissed her like that, yet it felt so right, and still did. The memories pleased and excited him, but they scared him, too. He didn't want to hurt Tina, in any way, but he also had to protect himself, too, himself and his sobriety. Even if he got the offer from the university, what was he supposed to do about Tina? What a mess.

When they reached the restaurant, he asked, "What would you like?"

"Just a malt and fries, like we talked about. Chocolate would be fine."

When did we talk about food? he wondered. Funny that he didn't remember the conversation. Tom walked over to place the order, his mind already starting to think about the portrait, mostly to keep his other thoughts in control. When would Masback call?

TINA WATCHED HIM at the counter, paying for their food. He was good-looking, even handsome in a rugged way. What was it that intrigued her so about him physically? He was not self-conscious, but he was preoccupied and self-contained, at times almost totally unaware of anything around him. How could that be appealing? Sometimes he was so absorbed in what he was doing, Tina got the feeling she could disappear and he wouldn't notice. Not for a while anyway. It wasn't just with the portrait, either. He was that way at the tide pools, watching the birds, staring at the ocean, or waiting for the whale to surface, and even here standing in line.

"Here you go," he said, returning to the table.

"Thanks."

They ate pretty much in silence, saying little more than the mundane.

"Pass the catsup, please."

"May I have the salt?"

On the walk back to his apartment, Tom held up his end of the conversation, but little more. They discussed the weather and the lack of parking. Tina sensed that he was only half here, even now, and that he could disappear again, almost without notice.

Where did he go when he disappeared? Deep within his own mind, she supposed, but he seemed to be a thousand miles away, at times even more. Where did he go and why? He would leave, and yet she knew that a part of him remained keenly observant. Even when apparently oblivious, he seemed to know exactly where all the people in the room where located, what they were doing. Their movements were recorded, but it was an automatic, machine process, like a robot. It chilled her to see it happening. When he came back to the present, the here and now, he was animated, friendly, and fun to be with. And so very gentle. But where did he go in the meanwhile?

AS TOM WORKED on the portrait, he felt himself getting sucked back into the process. Dr. Sallivant had prescribed art as therapy for him in the hospital, once he learned that Tom had dabbled in it as a kid. It had worked, and worked well, up to a point. Tom ended up drawing pictures of the things he could not talk about. Now, as he worked on Tina's portrait, Tom wondered if beginning it had been a mistake. No, it felt right, and the pastel was coming along well enough.

Still there were moments when a certain color of chalk triggered a memory, something from Vietnam, or a painting of Vietnam he had done in the hospital. He could concentrate those memories away. It was not quite what Sallivant had hoped for, but it worked for Tom. Until he had gotten fully into this portrait, Tom did not realize that Tina reminded him of a Vietnamese girl named Mei Lei. The name was all Tom ever knew about her because it was all she could whisper before she died. Tina and Mei Lei did not really look alike, other than their short, dark hair, but there was something about the shape of Tina's face that triggered the memory.

Triggered — that was how she had died, shot down in the street of her village by a fleeing Cong, just before the enemy escaped into the jungle. Had the man known the girl? Grown up with her, perhaps? Was he a relative? All those possibilities could be and had been true. Tom had seen every one of them happen.

"What's your name?" he had asked the young woman in Vietnamese, kneeling beside her.

"Mei Lei," she whispered.

Why her name had been so important to him, he no longer knew. The incident occurred early in his first tour of duty. Maybe he hadn't seen enough death, yet, to be hardened to it? She was too pretty and too young to die like that, in a dusty dirt street. Tom tried to will this memory away, but it was not an easy one to banish. The hand that held the chalk was shaking.

AFTER THEY RETURNED from the restaurant, Tina watched as Tom continued to work on the portrait. At first, he would sometimes hold up a pencil or a piece of chalk, sighting down it, as if he were measuring something on her face. But he smiled when he did that kind of thing, so she doubted it was serious. The real work was done when he went back and forth from the photograph to the paper. And the longer Tom worked, the less often he did those playful things. In fact, the less often he spoke, even. Tom had not said a single word in over an hour, now.

Tina had the strangest feeling that he did not need her here, not really. She was the subject of the portrait, but he really, truly did not need her. This knowledge created an empty feeling inside her. As the day began to turn into dusk, Tina continued to sit in the window, watching him work or looking out to the activities on the street. She had given up trying to make conversation because it just seemed to distract him. Tina grew quiet and a little sad as she remembered the events of the evening before, the pain and the fear. She tried to counter those memories with ones from this morning, but even those seemed to be fading fast.

From the window, Tina could see the end of the pier, just barely showing between two other buildings. Beyond the pier was a glimpse of the ocean, and beyond the ocean was a mere sliver of the great orange ball of the sun just beginning its descent. As the whole sky began to change colors, Tina wished she could be on the end of the pier, as far out as possible, in order to experience the sunset at its fullest, the glory of God's creation in reds and lavenders, unbelievable colors.

She started to call Tom over to look, but he was so engrossed in the portrait that she changed her mind. The whole sky had taken on a pinkish, iridescent cast, like a cosmic backlighting. Looking back and forth between Tom and the sunset, Tina wondered about the scene they were creating. Here she was, sitting in a window, looking out at the beauties of nature. There he was, sitting inside the apartment, creating art from a photograph. Where was the reality in this picture they formed? She was caught somewhere in the middle, but in the middle of what?

Suddenly, Tina came to a realization that was both profound and disturbing. She was lonely. Sitting in the same room with another human being, she was achingly alone! A few hours ago, they had kissed. Now this. It was not the silence, exactly. The quiet was actually comfortable. She could not stand people who had to talk all the time. That wore thin. But Tom was not here with her, not completely — that was the problem. A major portion of him was somewhere else, almost in a different dimension. His obsession with the picture, his concentration on it to the exclusion of her, these were symptoms of what she felt. Tina did not like this realization.

"Tom," she said, but it came out a whisper. She tried again, louder, "Tom." He did not respond but continued working.

This is silly, she thought. I'm just being nervous. The feeling will pass. It's just something leftover, some irrational fear. It'll go away in a minute. But it did not go. She grew increasingly edgy.

"Tom, please," she said, loud enough this time to break into his concentration if not through it.

"Yes. Just a minute."

But the minute stretched on and on. The longer she waited the more upset she became. Tina knew it made no sense, but she could feel her heart pounding in her chest.

"Now, Tom," she said with force, standing up, having to move, to do something other than just sit there, immobile.

"What's wrong?" Tom asked, obviously shocked at the vehemence in her voice.

Growing more and more nervous, feeling she had to do something — move, walk, something, anything — she suggested they stop for now and get ready for dinner, maybe some place on the highway. Partially, but only partially, breaking free from his concentration, Tom agreed.

"Sure, sounds good to me," he said, but immediately he looked back to the portrait.

"I'll go back to my place and see you there in an hour. Okay?" It was time to clean up and dress for dinner. No more portrait. No more isolation. She needed to move, to do something, but Tom had still not answered her. "Okay, Tom?" she tried again.

"What?" he asked, looking at her again, curiously, even blankly, for a minute, until her question seemed to register. "Oh yes, in an hour."

Walking home in the last light of the sunset, she thought the day through, the past five days, and the entanglements, the changes. Those few days seemed like absolute eons. So much had happened. So much and yet so little. It felt good just to move, to stretch. Sitting still for so long had tightened up the muscles in her neck and legs. She couldn't shake that feeling of loneliness she had experienced earlier. It was a profoundly powerful feeling, one that touched her so deeply that she couldn't quite name it. Loneliness only touched the surface. The feeling evoked the face of her father, and thinking of him made her feel sad, as it often did. Sadness and loneliness — how was that possible, when the day had started out so well?

Away from Tom, she remembered the good times from their hours together. In a strange way, the memories seemed to have more reality than the reality itself. Having just left him, she began to look forward to seeing him again. Perhaps they could take a swim later, unless it were too late or too dark? Who could tell? A nice possibility. A romantic moonlight swim? He had kissed her, hadn't he?

TINA WAITED THE FULL HOUR, then gave him ten minutes more. This time she did not even get irritated; instead, she became more deeply saddened. She walked back to his place and climbed the stairs, already knowing what she would find. She could see him through the front window and knew that the door would still be open, just as she had left it. Tom had not moved from the portrait. He was still working on it, steadily, mechanically. Tina stood there watching him for several minutes before going in. What place was there for her in this man's life? In his consciousness? Not her picture, but her. The real her. She felt herself putting up the familiar barriers again.

They were the same barriers she had used with her father, every other weekend, on the court-designated visits, those mandated father-and-daughter times. Good at first, then more and more strained as his girlfriends began. She knew now that there had always been girlfriends. The lady in the laundry room was one, as were all those other

Bathshebas who showed up on their father-and-daughter weekends.

Little by little, Tina and her father grew apart, guarded with each other, until now they no longer spoke much. He lived out of state and had for several years, but that was not the reason, just the excuse. Her father had no time for her in his busy life; he never had. He had more time for the girlfriends, an endless string of them, getting younger as he got older. Tom's self-absorption, what she saw as his inconsiderateness, caused Tina to raise the walls. It was a familiar feeling. Rejection.

Quietly she entered the room, walls up. Tom was so engrossed that he didn't seem to hear her open the door and walk in. Tina recognized the bizarre irony of the scene, even as she entered it. Almost surrealistic, somehow. He was so occupied with the portrait of the woman that he had no time for the woman herself. It felt so damned familiar that she wanted to cry. Her father had always liked to show her off to his friends, but he had little real time for her. He liked having a daughter, but it was more for his own image than for the person she was. As Tina walked toward Tom, he shifted a little in acknowledgment of her presence. Yet she knew that on some critical level, he did not even realize she had ever left. Tina stepped to where she could look over his shoulder at the pad on which he was working.

My God! The portrait was good! The shock of seeing it almost broke her strange mood.

"Oh, Tom," she whispered.

The charcoal outline was finished and a big portion of the colored chalk had been applied. Tina thought it was halfway done but had no real way to tell. She guessed that Tom had not moved since she left but had continued working, obsessed. She watched as he continued to work, even now, applying color with his thumb.

Strange, Tina thought! She put her hand up to her neck, feeling for her grandmother's crucifix, given to her on Confirmation Sunday, years ago. She was not wearing it, now, and was pretty sure she had not worn it for several days because she never did when planning on going to the beach. The cross was in its velvet box in her dresser drawer. Yet here it was on her neck in the portrait. Unfinished, uncolored, but clearly her grandmother's crucifix. When could Tom have seen it? She could not remember. Tina double-checked the photograph he was using as a model, but she had been wearing pearls that day. What an eerie feeling! Her Grams had died three years before. Seeing the cross was like hearing a whisper from the other world.

Slowly Tom came back to the present, apologizing when he realized what he had done, forgetting they were going out. "I'm sorry, Tina. Guess I just got carried away. It won't take me a minute to get dressed."

He stood up, temporarily blocking her view of the portrait, but then he bent over for a couple of last-minute touches, even before walking into the other room to clean up and dress for dinner. He did not look at her again, walking away as if he were oblivious to her presence. Tina watched him, sensing that Tom had no idea of how late he was. It might have been ten minutes or two hours, for all he knew. His apology had been a form effort, not really taking into account her feelings. Did he even remember that he was to have gone to her place to meet? Once Tom left the room, Tina looked back to the chair, only to find that he had closed the tablet, again hiding the portrait, even though he must have known she had seen it. Or did he even realize she had returned, really? Tina felt her walls going up even higher, saddened and confused by feelings that were all too familiar.

In the pocket of her coat, Tina found an old tissue. When she walked into the kitchen area to drop it into the trash can, she noticed a phone number there, written on a paper towel wrapper. It was the local prefix, followed by 4-7-5-9. Somehow it was familiar, but she could not identify it. Shrugging her shoulders, she walked back into the living room to wait for Tom. She sat in front of the covered portrait.

TOM LET HER PICK the restaurant. After all, Tina was so much more familiar with the area than he. He suggested that she choose a nice place, somewhere they could celebrate. He remembered using that very word, celebrate, but now he wondered why? Celebrate what? The portrait? The interview? Their being together? He was almost sorry he had opened his mouth. Tina did not look celebratory. She was distracted, silent, but wasn't that understandable? Who could blame her? After all that had happened? A good meal and some live music would perk her up. Tom made a promise to himself that he would be good company for her tonight. Lord knows, he was distracted enough himself. Working on the portrait had been good for him, though. At least, he had stopped thinking for a few hours.

What was he going to do? Everything had gone well at the university, even the impromptu lecture. The ten or twelve students who showed up, probably draftees, had asked some good questions. Twice he had confessed that he did not know, but would think about it and get back to them, if he could. The students actually seemed pleased with his responses. Maybe they had never heard a teacher admit he did not know. At the end of the evening, Dr. Masback congratulated him, saying that everything was in the bag. But Tom would not know for sure until the committee met and voted, tomorrow morning, most likely. Saturday morning, that is. Without the teaching fellowship, there would be no schooling. He could not afford it otherwise.

Tom looked over at Tina who was walking by his side. What was he going to do about them? He and Tina? Tom had no answer. If things were different, if he got the job. If, if, if — his mind swam, until they reached the restaurant. Tina entered silently as he held the door open for her. They had hardly talked on the way over.

TINA WAS SURPRISED when they ordered because Tom asked for iced tea. She had already ordered a mixed drink for herself, still a new experience that made her a little nervous, even while pleasing her. Only three months since her last birthday, when she could finally do this legally. They could be celebrating her twenty-first birthday, her coming of age. The actual evening of her birthday had fallen on a school night, but even more, it was the night before a big exam, so she just had a single glass of wine with a couple of girlfriends. Tonight she wanted and needed a drink. No excuses offered or given. Unlike many of her friends, she seldom drank at all. She could not even remember the last time she had. Perhaps a beer a week ago?

Celebrate, he had said. But would he keep her company and have a drink? No. Once again she saw his face with the dancer from Pandora's Box. He drank. She had seen him drunk. She could still see the neon light blinking on and off over his face. Or was it her father's face? She had never found the time to go by that street again, to see if Pandora's was even there. She lifted her drink only to find that it was already empty. Good! She would get drunk tonight. That would show him! Show whom? Her father did not need to see it. He was usually so drunk himself that he would not even notice. Show Tom?

"Do you want another?" Tom asked.

Tina noted the strange look on his face. What was it? Concern? Disgust? Confusion? How dare he look at me like that! she thought. "Yes, please," she said aloud, as sweetly as she could make it sound, smiling broadly. She liked this feeling. Daring. Bravado. Pull out all the stops. What the hell. She could not even believe these were her thoughts.

TOM PICKED UP the glass and walked to the bar, where he ordered her another drink. Standing there was a familiar sensation, one from the past. He had not done this for almost a year. Why didn't he just have the waitress bring the drink? For some reason, he'd wanted to get away from Tina. Not because she ordered a drink. Good grief, she could have one if she wanted. Booze was his problem, not hers. He would already know if she had a drinking problem. There had been no signs of that, and he should be able to tell, if anyone could. What then? Some other reason. Was he getting too close? Pushing her? Was that it? Irrationally, Tom wanted to walk away and just keep going. Why? What was going on here? It made no sense. Was she getting too close to him? They had enjoyed a good day. Last night had been horrible for Tina, but today was good. He enjoyed it, so did she, but now she was acting so strangely. What was wrong?

"Tom, is that you?" one of the cocktail waitresses asked, stopping in front of him. "It's me, Martha, from the Tuesday meeting. Remember?"

"Oh, sure," Tom responded, finally recognizing her. Martha was dressed in a skimpy cocktail outfit. When they'd met in the church hall, she'd been wearing street clothes. Tom stood up straight, ready to greet her, but not sure what was proper in the restaurant.

"Don't look so shocked, Tom," she said, giving him a quick hug, as bouncy and uninhibited as he remembered her. "I only serve the cocktails, I don't drink them myself. Or is it the outfit?" she asked, joking with him by pirouetting in front of him. "A job's a job. Besides the pay's good and I can still get to my classes during the day."

"No, Martha" he started out, flustered for words, "it's just that I didn't recognize you at first. It's good to see you."

"You, too, Tom, but I have to turn in this order. Friday's are always like this — busy, busy, busy. See you later. At a meeting maybe?"

"Right. See you later," he said, watching as she took off across the floor at a quick walk, almost a trot.

THROUGH THE ARCHWAY into the bar, Tina could see Tom clearly. She was watching when the cocktail waitress gave him a hug and a kiss on the cheek. It jolted her to the very bottoms of her feet. Was it the same woman? The dancer from Pandora's? The woman never turned her way, so Tina could not see her face, but the pose and her outfit — everything about the scene triggered memories of what she had seen in the alley outside of Pandora's Box. It must be the same dancer. Who else would Tom know that well, in just a week?

While she sat there in a state of mild shock, Tina saw Ed as he walked into the restaurant, his appearance adding to her state of mind. *Oh please, God,* she begged, *don't let him notice me.* When she saw Ed head for the bar, she breathed a little easier, until she realized that Tom was still standing there. What, if anything, could she do? What did she want to do? Almost paralyzed, she moved the chair back just an inch, sensing the inevitable.

As she started to rise, Ed did look over and see her. He raised a hand in recognition, almost a wave, but when he looked closer and seemed to notice her expression, the hand dropped. Tina could imagine the look on her own face, just by what she was feeling inside.

Ed froze, mouthing the words, "Tina, please?"

"No, Ed. Don't come near me." Tina was not sure if she had mouthed the response, willed it, or said it out loud, maybe even shouted it. She did know that she had shaken her head in a no, an absolute no.

"Okay," he answered, from across the room, and nodded, looking defeated. Then he turned and started into the bar.

Was it Ed who'd been phoning her? she wondered again. She'd never really asked him or accused him, but it did seem to fit with his following her around. Thinking of the crank calls reminded Tina of the familiar phone number in Tom's trash can — 4-7-5-9 — and suddenly she remembered where she had seen the number before. It was Maggie's. Her so-called friend.

TOM FOUND HIMSELF using the mirrors behind the bar to case the room. It was an old habit, partly military, partly alcoholic. He did not recognize Ed at first, having only seen him that first day on the beach, most clearly when his hair was wet. As the man stood there, just an image in a mirror, Tom realized Ed was staring at the back of his head. Tom knew it was the same football player, ex-boyfriend — big, strong, blond. When Ed started toward him in the mirror, Tom prepared himself, physically, mentally. He was instantly combat-ready, his mind measuring the distance, planning the attack.

As Ed came almost within range, he slowed, then stopped. Tom froze, relaxed to all appearances, but every muscle was ready. In the mirror, he watched the confusion on the other man's face. Why was he hesitating? Tom stared at the image behind the bar. The man was crying. He was still in control, but the tears were real. They were trickling down both cheeks. Ed took the final two steps and reached out to touch Tom's shoulder. Tom saw it in the mirror, even as he felt it. Slowly, he turned his head to look at the other man.

"I'm sorry," was all Ed could say at first. "I'm so very sorry. I never meant to hurt Tina. If I could undo it, I would, but now it's too late. She won't talk to me, and I can't blame her. I really messed things up. Would you just tell her for me? That I'm sorry?"

When Tom nodded, Ed tentatively offered his hand. Tom was surprised, but, after a short pause, he took the man's hand and shook it. Ed said he was sorry once more, thanked Tom, promised to leave Tina alone, and then turned and walked away, dignified and proud. Tom watched his every step, not in the mirror this time, but half-turned, standing at the bar.

For a while, Tom remained there, willing his body to relax. One minute he had been ready to tear the man apart, but now he felt sorry for him. It was not just pity, though. After all, the big ape had hurt Tina. He deserved whatever he got. But obviously the man was crying because he cared for Tina. Tom actually felt a growing respect for the man. It had taken real guts to do that, to make amends with public tears streaming down his face. Tom almost envied him, not being able to remember the last time he had cried like that. When he wept for Bruce, it had been sobs — helpless, out-of-control sobs. Sometimes he wept in his own sleep. He could feel the tears on the pillow, later. But Tom couldn't just cry because he was sad. He wished he could, many times, but he could not. The tears came only in his dreams, now. Finally, he picked up the drink, pocketed his change, after automatically leaving a tip, and walked back to the table. She was gone.

TOM WENT STRAIGHT TO HER HOUSE, running almost the whole way, holding himself just barely in check. He retraced the same route they had used getting to the restaurant, but he never saw Tina ahead of him. When he reached her place, it was dark. Not even a porch light. She could not have gotten there ahead of him and already be inside. He was certain of it. But where was she? At first, back at the restaurant, he had not been worried, thinking she might have gone to the rest room, but as time passed, Tom felt a growing sense that something was wrong, seriously wrong. Their waitress had checked the rest room, looking at him like he was crazy for asking.

"No, sir, she isn't in there."

"Are you sure?"

"Very sure. I remember the lady, and she is not in there."

Checking the rest of the restaurant took only a second. It was not that big a place. She had gone, just walked out, leaving him there. But why? She must have seen him and Ed at the bar — that was the only answer he could think of —

but nothing happened, so why would she leave? Good Lord, he thought, the guy had almost raped her. Maybe she expected him to smash Ed? Was that it? For that matter, why hadn't he smashed the guy? Tom still didn't know the answer to that one. He had been ready to do it. If Tom couldn't answer the question, how could she? Had she fled into the night because he'd let her down, again? Maybe it was just that simple. Tom had no idea what kind of car she drove, or even where it would be parked. Her place did not have a garage. If she parked on the street, the car could be anywhere in a three-block radius — The Shore had that bad of a parking problem.

Tom waited for her a long time, willing his mind to be still. Across the street from her house, leaning up against a tree, he waited. Once a bird stirred above his head, fluttering its wings. Traffic came and went, sometimes with the same car circling the block several times, trying to find a parking place. She did not return. Tom did not leave until after he had frightened a senior citizen woman half to death. She was walking her little dog, carrying a piece of newspaper with her for the animal's mess. The woman was dressed in clothes so dark that Tom did not even see her at first, not until she said something to the animal. They were a house away then but coming closer. When they got within five or six feet, the dog decided to use the tree Tom was standing under, but it began to yip and growl, sensing his presence.

"Quiet," Tom said, trying to hush the animal.

The woman was totally unprepared and almost fell over in fear, crossing herself and mumbling something in a foreign tongue that he could not understand, something in Old European that sounded like, "Madre."

"I'm sorry," Tom said, trying to apologize, but the old woman just tottered down the street, muttering to herself.

He could not blame her for being frightened. Late at night, in the dark, he had tried to apologize, but she had every right to be terrified. Finally, Tom sighed, deciding to give up the vigil, and started walking back to his own place. What good could he do, standing there in the dark? As he walked, Tom felt an immense, fog-like sadness threatening to engulf him. Carefully he forced the feeling into submission even as he continued to walk through it. Somehow he had let Tina down. He couldn't blame her for running off and leaving him. Perhaps, it was better this way?

AS SHE CONTINUED to walk on the beach, Tina replayed the restaurant scene in her mind, over and over. Heart pounding, she had left the table. Once out the door, she promised herself, I'll never look back, so help me, God! Did the phone number mean that Tom was seeing Maggie behind her back? The pain of that thought was indescribable. Once again, her mind flashed on the picture of Tom and Maggie kissing in the doorway to Pandora's Box, the way she had dreamed it, but that thought also invoked the image of her father kissing the blond Bathsheba in the laundry room. My God, the cocktail waitress had hugged him, right there in the bar. She was probably the one kissing Tom in the alley. But how could all of these things be possible? They couldn't! None of this was making a bit of sense. Tina knew that, but she could not stop the thoughts or the feelings from coming.

Rationally, Tina knew that Tom and she had spent almost every minute of the past few days together. No, that was not true. What about that whole day he had disappeared? He said he was at the university, but had he really spent that day and night in bed with Maggie? Without a doubt, Tina knew her friend would have slept with Tom. Her friend of what? Some ten years or more? Tina distinctly remembered the picture of Maggie on the beach and what she'd said about Tom.

"Where's he off to today?" she had asked. "Is he still in town?"

Tina could still see the way Maggie had stretched, in that languid way of hers, like a cat in heat. Had she known the whole time where Tom was and where he had just been — with her, in bed? How she must have laughed to herself over Tina's response.

"Yes, he's still here."

Tina had said the words hoping they were true, but they mocked her now, as she looked across the room at Tom's back, standing there in the bar.

Yes, he was still here, and so was Ed.

Seeing Tom and Ed standing at the bar like that was just too much. Her rapist and her betrayer, except that Ed hadn't raped her, nor did she really believe that Tom had betrayed her, in spite of all the "evidence" — none of it fit with the man she knew, Tom, or the man she thought she knew. All her suspicions came down to a quick hug from a cocktail waitress and a phone number thrown into a trash can. One flimsy piece of paper. On top of everything else, Tina had spent the whole summer looking forward to her student teaching, getting ready to know and teach a classroom full of children. Just a few days to go and here she was, emotionally tied to two grown-up children. It was like watching the Shoot-Out at the OK Corral.

Let them slug it out! she remembered thinking. A fistfight would be so macho! Have at it! Once she had liked Ed, though she had never loved him. A week ago they had even been a couple, or sort of a couple. Good grief! They might have gone to a prom together. Now what? How could she even be in the same room with him? She had tried to forgive Ed and had succeeded, for the most part. But she would have nothing more to do with him. She did not need that kind of violence in her life. Violence masquerading as love.

As she continued to walk on the beach, replaying the evening, Tina knew she was not being honest, not completely. Her jealousy over Maggie was ridiculous — all based on a phone number in a trash can. She was no longer even sure that it was Maggie's number, besides which it had been tossed aside, trashed. Tina knew she had run out into the night for reasons beyond some imagined jealousy or because two guys were going to fight each other. It was not that simple. Actually, the scene had evoked multiple old memories from her childhood, one being the picture of her father in the laundry room with Bathsheba, another the picture of him in a horrible barroom fight. Part of her had run from those memories and was still running from them. She was ten when her father took her to his regular bar during a visitation weekend. The bartender was not happy about it. He did not want her there.

"Hey, Dave, get the kid out of here."

"Come on, Bobby. What's she gonna hurt? You serve food. She can be here."

"It's not right, Dave."

But her father had insisted, parking her on a stool in a dark corner while he walked around, greeting his friends. One was a woman he kissed and talked to for what seemed an eternity. When he finally returned, her father bought her a Shirley Temple to drink. Tina could still see the drink as it was handed to her, the glass and the twist of orange peel.

"Here you go, honey," the bartender said, but she was still afraid of him and said nothing in reply. The man had a funny Southern accent. Tina could still remember that.

How the fight broke out, she didn't know and had never been able to recall. Something to do with a bet over a pool game, she thought, but who could be certain, especially after all these years? She had looked over in time to see her father hit another man, full-force, in the face. Then all hell broke loose. She had seen boys fight in the playground before, but this was different, very different. Bottles were broken, chairs and tables turned over, while people shouted and cheered. The fight ended with her father flat on his back, being pummeled by the man he had hit. Over and over, the bigger man hit her daddy while she screamed for him to stop. Finally, a couple of the men dragged the fighters apart, but Tina could not stop crying, in the bar and all the way back to her father's apartment.

"Stop your tears, for God's sake," he said, holding a paper towel to his lip. "I'm all right. It takes a better man than him to put me down."

Tina had never forgotten that day. Since then, she could not watch prize fights on television, and she even had to close her eyes in movies when scenes got too violent.

In the restaurant, standing at the exit, she had watched as Ed neared Tom. She feared for Ed, big as he was, but she could not stay in the restaurant, not even to warn him. She could not get caught up in the middle of this. She was even having trouble breathing. Still, she paused in the doorway, drawn to the scene. Tom would kill him. Ed outweighed

Tom by fifty pounds, but Tom would surely kill him. She had no idea what horrible, primitive dimension Tom had survived and still carried within him, but she sensed what he could do from his dreams, his demons. There was an icy coldness about him that disturbed her, even terrified her. It confused her just as badly that he could be so wonderfully gentle, too. A total overwhelming paradox. She recognized this chaos, now, as being the same confused feelings she experienced as a child.

More pictures flashed through her mind, like scenes in a kaleidoscope. Growing up, she had lived in just that kind of a paradox. Her father's rages, his drinking. Apologies followed by the good times. Then his women had begun. More arguments followed by happy birthday parties. The flower beds dug up, vandalized, violated, but then a nice vacation trip. Little by little, the violent bad outweighed the peaceful good, until all she could remember was violence. Broken furniture and broken glass. The divorce. Her mother's breakdown and then her rages, her depressions. It was too, too much, remembering. Violence terrified Tina, immobilized her. She had to get out of the restaurant. She had to. But still she continued to watch.

The way Tom stood at the bar reminded her of her father, over the years, the way he always stood near the wet bar in whatever apartment he was currently renting. If she were asked to describe her father, it would be in that very pose: a sophisticated male in an oaken setting, with the phone numbers of a dozen women in his pocket.

Growing up in such a violent household, Tina had learned to control her own emotions with great care. She wanted to run now, but she could not step through the door. She felt frozen, helpless. She could see Ed in profile, see the tears on his cheeks. At first, she could only see the back of Tom's head, until he turned to look at Ed. Watching Tom's expression, Tina knew then that there would be no fight. She felt relief, but it was only for the moment.

My God, there they stood, shaking hands! Her rapist and her betrayer. But that thought was nonsense. Ed had not raped her, she knew that. Tom had not, could not betray her, she knew that. Yet, the scene made her feel both furious and helpless. Betrayed and abandoned. She was like a child's puppet with the strings being yanked. Dancing. Jerking. Once again, Tina suddenly saw a picture of her father and Bathsheba kissing under the laundry room light. All the old confusion.

"Why was Daddy kissing that lady, Mommy?" she had asked. "Why?"

"I don't know, dear," her mother answered, holding her, as they both cried. "I don't know."

Shaking hands, the two men were being oh so civilized in dividing up the spoils — her, Tina, the prize. When Ed turned to walk away, Tina stepped through the door, moved left toward the ocean, and began to run. *Enough of this!* she thought. *It was just too damn much!* She ran down the steps, until she was outside the glow of the street lights. She could hear the ocean ahead, but she could barely see her feet in front of her. She was forced to slow down when she reached the sand, but she continued on, struggling and trudging toward the water, crying all the way.

Tina ran until she was tired. Then she walked and walked and walked. She moved to the hard-packed, wet sand because it was easier going. When the moon disappeared behind a cloud, she lost sight of the waterline and ended up soaking her feet, shoes and all. And to think that she had fantasized about a romantic midnight swim! She took off her shoes and carried them under her arm, continuing to walk. On and on. It was really dark now. She could no longer see the moon clearly, and hardly any stars were visible, either. The sky was full of clouds. Dark ominous clouds.

Chapter Six: Saturday

IT WAS CALLED AN ORATORY, as she recalled. Just a small chapel, off the main cathedral, but it was always open, always available as a place of worship, a place of prayer. She knew it was late but had not realized it was after midnight, until she got to the church. Tentatively she tried the door and found it open. She sighed in gratitude. How long had she walked? A couple of hours, at least. Still barefoot, she genuflected and crossed herself. God will forgive the shoes. He would also have to forgive her bare head. Tina did not have a handkerchief she could use to cover herself. Though it was no longer required or even suggested, she still liked the old ways. Latin in the liturgy. Fish on Friday, too. Mostly the rules and rituals of the Church comforted her, but tonight they frustrated her because she could not do them right, the way she wanted. Now, just when she needed the familiar rites, her shoes were wet and she had no handkerchief. Always before, she had come to church prepared, a regularly scheduled mass with other people present. Tonight she was alone, coming to God out of need. Seeking God because she felt so terribly alone. Still craving ritual, she slid into saying the Hail Mary three times, and then an Our Father, ending with a fervent Amen. It shall be so. God's promise. Late at night. Eternal mystery.

Over and over, her mind replayed the events of the previous day — the beach, the kisses, the portrait, always ending with the scene at the restaurant. Why had she run? Even now she could feel her stomach tightening with the beginning of a panic attack, an old reaction that she thought was a thing of the past. Such attacks had occurred all the way back to when she was a small child. Times of stress like tests at school would affect her this same way, no matter how well she was doing in the course. The reaction was emotional, not intellectual, and its source was rooted way back in her childhood. After her father moved out of the house, she developed a fear of sleeping alone, even of being alone, in her room. She would crawl into bed with her mother anytime she was allowed. They would often cry themselves to sleep.

"No, Tina," her mother finally told her when she was six or so. "You have to start sleeping in your own bed, now."

"Mommy, please," Tina had begged, "I don't want to be alone."

The worst was when her father filed for divorce and announced that he was going to remarry. Her mother went into acute depressions, alternating with rages. How old had she been then? Tina wondered. Eight or nine? Her parents had been separated for several years by then, but she and her mother still talked about when her father would come home to live with them. Tina understood now that her mother had fostered that belief in her, long past any hope of its coming to pass. She could still remember the day her Aunt Kathy had picked her up from school and told her the news.

"Tina," she said, "Your mother is very sick. You are going to come live with us for a while, just until she gets well and can come home."

"What's wrong with her?" she asked.

"She's just sad, honey. Very sad."

For six months she lived with her cousins, in their room, listening to them whisper about what was really wrong with her mother.

"She's crazy, a loony."

"She is not!" Tina would reply, defending her mother. "She's just sad."

"Loony, loony, loony," they teased her.

Tina moved into a new school, right in the middle of the year. All her old friends were a hundred miles away, and she had a very hard time making new ones, she remembered, probably because she was so withdrawn. Tina could still feel the miasma of overwhelming loneliness that engulfed her then. She learned the word later — miasma — and never forgot it because the word so perfectly described her situation. Alone, all alone. A cloud of loneliness seemed to spread over her entire childhood. Even after her mother got out of the hospital and they went home, Tina still feared that her mother would leave again. She feared it for a long, long time.

Once, Tina had stayed with her grandmother, Grandma Claire — Clara in German — her mother's mother, but Grams died the year before her mother's breakdown. Tina still remembered the month at her grandmother's as the happiest time of her childhood. She felt safe, loved and protected. Tina could tell her Grams anything and still be kissed and hugged for it. She was such a special lady. So tall, with pure white hair.

Not until Grace came into her life a few years later, did Tina have a friend to confide in completely, someone to share her fears with. Tina told her all of it, everything. Grace would always listen, treating what Tina told her seriously, but Grace would never let her stay in the dumps very long.

"Lighten up, Tina," Grace would say. "It's time to go. On your feet. Time's awasting, and life is wonderful. What are we gonna do today?"

Grace always had a way of lifting her spirits, making her laugh. She wished that Grace were with her now.

Tina stayed in the chapel for an hour or so, praying and thinking. She left only when her solitude was disturbed by an old woman who struggled her way down to a front pew, where she knelt in prayer, looking upset, troubled. Sitting in the back, Tina watched her. Dressed in black. Old world appearance. Italian? Bulgarian? What was she doing here so late at night? Tina would sometimes go to an early mass, especially if she had something planned for the weekend. She had grown used to seeing the old women, dressed in black, at those early morning services. Did they ever sleep? Or did they keep eternal vigil for the past? The Dead? Lost children. Lost dreams. Faith of the Ages. Would that be her someday? A lonely, old woman in black? Solitary? Isolated? Wasn't that her already, even now? Alone, seeking an answer, but fearing the knowledge, she looked to the altar. Wings of the doves. All the blessed saints. God help me.

TOM DID NOT RUN this morning. Instead, he started working on the portrait the minute he woke up. He did not even take time to eat. This was the first pastel he had done since the hospital, but he had still brought the materials with him, to the beach, thinking he could get back into it. A relaxing hobby. Except it didn't relax him. Never had. Once he got started on a painting, he was obsessed to see it finished. An artist? He had once hoped to be, but now daydreams of himself, dressed like Gauguin, painting naked native women, was just too silly to take seriously. Here he was in a tropical paradise, right now, but he was no Gauguin. Nor had he seen any naked women. The thought made his skin flush because his mind leaped to Tina whose face he was painting at that very moment. He could feel himself blushing. How did he think of Tina? He did not visualize her naked. At times he saw her like a younger sister, at other times like a companion. Why didn't he think of her as a sexual being, a possible sexual partner? He was no fantasy knight in shining armor, nor was she a fairy tale princess in a castle. Why did he avoid thinking of her as a sexual being, as a real woman? Was it something to do with his own hangups?

What about sex? During the early months of his sobriety, sex had been no problem because he was completely shut down, physically. Nada, zip. Wayne said it was normal. It happened to lots of men. The good news was that normal functioning came back. His making a joke out of it helped, and he was right. Function returned, suddenly. He just woke up one morning and there it was. Eventually he tried sex with a couple of women in the program. The first time, he was terrified that he would not be able to perform, but everything had worked out, thank God. He did not continue with either of the women, partly because he was not supposed to get involved this early in sobriety, but it had been more than that. Sex was not enough, somehow. He wanted more. But more what? Love? For the first time in his life, he had women friends, women in the program. They were like sisters to him, the sisters he never had. You couldn't sleep with your sisters, so he had been celibate for months now. Him? Women-were-a-dime-a-dozen Tom? Use-them-like-Kleenex Tom? Celibate? The thought made him laugh, but it was true.

Tom stood and stepped back from the portrait. He was getting very close now. Almost finished. If necessary, he would force himself to stop working on the picture before he overworked it. He was a perfectionist, half-gift, half-curse. Who could have guessed that he would end this week by working on a pastel portrait of a woman he had met on the beach? Gauguin indeed. She was sweet. A nice girl. Tina deserved good things. He hoped she would get them. Yes. It was now time to quit. He could work on the upper left corner a little more and her lips, perhaps. But if he did, he would then be working on her shoulders, her cheeks, the shadows on her hairline, her eyes. He found himself getting aroused and willed the reaction away, ashamed of himself. With a last glance at the portrait, he headed for the door. He would leave her alone. He would run. He could always shave and shower later on. One last glance at her eyes, and he headed for the beach.

ALL MORNING LONG it had threatened to rain, with the whole sky grey and brooding. Looking out the window of the Laundromat, she knew it would rain today. Just a matter of time. Tina had slept fitfully. Late as it had been when she got home, she woke at her usual hour. Running on nervous energy, she did her daily chores. The Laundromat was just down the street, on the corner. It was always busier on Saturdays, but she had no trouble getting machines, arriving so early. The last load was in the drier. In another twenty minutes, it would be done. She could fold it and walk home. When she first entered the laundry that morning, Tina had the strangest urge to kneel and cross herself. The machines were lined up in rows, on both sides, like pews. The front doors to the Laundromat were double wide, centered in the front wall, just like the doors to a cathedral. An aisle ran down the middle, all the way to the back wall. Where the altar should be, on that far wall, across from the doors, was a machine dispenser for soap. The dark blue plastic looked like marble in the early light. Put in a quarter and wash your sins away. Such sacrilege! Where did she get thoughts like that? She smiled. It was just a little sin. Clever really. Wash your sins away. Still she banished the thought. It wasn't that funny.

She was just tired. Much too little sleep lately. Forget the lately part. She was still trying not to think about the last few days. Not yet. Too early. Tina looked around the room. People-watching was a great hobby. Most of the customers were her age. College students. Some young mothers, but usually couples did not try to raise families in The Shore. This was a young person's town. Paradise. Eden. Some Eden, she thought, smiling to herself, as she looked at the mess on the floor. Paper cups. Empty cartons of soap. A weekly ritual of cleansing. Purification.

"Are you done with the washer, dear?" one of the exceptions asked her, an older woman, dressed in a sweater and pants, under a hooded rain coat.

"Yes, I am. Help yourself."

"Guess we're all here trying to beat the rain?" the woman added, making small talk.

"It sure looks like a storm, doesn't it?" Tina responded.

"Thunder and lightning would be my guess. All my synthetics are clinging. Lots of static in the air," the woman said, moving off.

Static in the air? Maybe that was part of her edginess? Tina wondered. She thought it was just lack of sleep. No, that was a cop-out. The lack of sleep was from the edginess of the night before, the events at the restaurant.

Tina thought of Tom, no longer trying to keep thoughts of him at bay, outside her consciousness. What did these feelings really have to do with him? Her jealousy made no sense. Tom hadn't slept with Maggie, nor had he fought with Ed. And Ed had not raped her. Instead, he apologized and cried like a baby. All these fears were in her mind, where they butted up against so many other upsetting things. Next year would be her senior year in college. She would graduate, then go out into the world, a full adult, with all the rights and privileges thereto. Responsibilities. She had always been responsible, probably a little too responsible. But this teaching would be different. Twenty babies given into her care, to teach, shape, mold, guide, direct. Could she do it?

No wonder she was a mess! Some major changes were rushing straight at her, like a freight train. This was the year she had been working toward. Student teacher — it had a nice ring to it. One more year and she would be a real teacher. Funny choice of words. Wasn't she real now? Last night, in the chapel, she had prayed and prayed. Every prayer she had ever memorized — Ave Maria, St. Francis, all of the regulars. Francis and the animals, the birds. She had seen a statue of him just the other day. Where had it been? Would the Church ever ordain a woman? Nuns were leaving their various orders in droves. She read about it in the newspaper, just last week. Once she had wanted to be a nun. Didn't every little girl Catholic, every little Catholic girl — how would you say that? Neither way sounded right. She could ask Tom. He was in English. If she ever saw him again. Why had she run from him the night before? Would she see him today? Could she see him? When? As a child, she had fantasized being a nun. The wife of Christ. A virgin forever doing good in this world. It held a powerful attraction. How old had she been. Eight? Ten? Twelve? She never told anyone, except Grace.

"Sister Tina, Sister Tina," her friend repeated, trying it out for sound. "No, they'll just change your name."

"No, they won't. They don't do that."

"Of course, they do," Grace had responded. "You don't think Sister George was born that way, do you?"

They both laughed over that, imagining the sister being called George as a child. Grace had taken Tina seriously because she too thought of being a nun. Grace told her so. In time, the desire went away. Perhaps when her parents divorced? No, it was after that, but not by much. She couldn't remember for sure, but an old idea from the past went through her mind. She must have thought it, once, and believed it. Could the daughter of divorced people be a nun? Or would she carry the blame and the sins of the parents, like a disease, to her grave?

The buzzer went off again, for the second time, she suspected. Maybe a nap when she got home? Tina thought she would be too tired and confused to make it through the day, otherwise. She folded and hung the last load of drying. The smell of clean clothes was nice. Warm and fragrant. As usual, she put her lingerie under something else in the basket. A folded towel. Or a blouse. Why not put it right on top for everyone to see? Black lace bra. French cut panties. Maybe in crimson. Cause a stir. But she owned nothing like that. Her friends reveled in that kind of stuff. Racy underwear. Typical gifts for a bridal shower. All her lingerie was white, functional, washable, and practical. What was the name of that place in Hollywood? Frederick's? What kind of people worked in a business like that? Probably not Catholics. The guilt would eat you up. But maybe not all Catholics felt that way. Just ones like her. The devout. The old women in black. Mea culpa, mea culpa.

On the wall across the room, a poster caught her eye. A woman with her hair blowing in the wind was standing with her arms spread out wide. It was an advertisement for something in a box, detergent probably, but the pose reminded Tina of the famous painting of Ophelia, Hamlet's sister in Shakespeare's play. In that painting, Ophelia looks as if she is floating in a pool of water, until you realize she is actually under the water, drowned. Dead, like Mary Jo Kopechne. Abandoned. Alone. Forgotten. A sadness came over Tina as she thought about the last couple of days, but her thoughts were more like images than organized ideas. Library books, a torn blouse, a kiss on the beach, and a crucifix on a painting of her, a painting that made her feel lonely and forgotten, like Ophelia and all drowned women calling out for justice.

As she walked the half block home, lugging the basket, she looked at the sky several times. It was definitely going to rain. The wash was more difficult to handle all folded up. She carried the hangers in her left hand, the hooks looped over two fingers. The same hand also held one side of the basket. Maybe she should get one of those wire pull carts? The kind old ladies use for groceries and laundry? The old ladies in black. She wasn't ready for that, not yet. The strain on her arms felt good, like a mini-workout. She felt surprisingly healthy, tired but healthy. A nap might still be nice. Then she could start making plans for the rest of the day. Would she ever see him again? Would he forgive her for running out? Who knew? Whom? Or was it Who?

TOM RAN FULL-OUT for the last quarter mile. The four-forty was called a run sometimes, other times a sprint. In high school track, he had hated the quarter mile. As a long distance runner, he did them in practice for speed and kick, but they were sheer torture. Just look at the faces of the runners as they finish: Some are dying. Some are straining, as if their feet were turned to stone. Some are neutral, eyes flat, the faces of running zombies. None are smiling. Ever. Once Tom asked a quarter-miler why he chose that race.

"Believe me, I didn't choose it," he responded, "the race chose me. I'm way too slow for the sprints and much too smart for the distances. How about you?" he asked, with a smile, knowing Tom was a miler.

"Same thing," he responded. "Too slow for the sprints."

"Uh huh?"

"Oh, yes. And I always feel so much smarter after running a mile," Tom finished.

"Sure you do, and twice as smart after a two-mile race, I suppose?"

Whether it were smart or not, he did not know, but running had become habitual. He always felt better afterward, just like he did now, walking it off, slowly cooling down. Tom had finally learned not to overdo his workouts. Like everything else, he could get so obsessive, so caught up in running, that he would damage his body. Last time it was his shins. Now he followed a set distance schedule, just so many miles a week. He would miss the running far too much if he had to lay off for any reason. Perhaps he was finally learning moderation? Fat chance.

When Tom came to the pier, he climbed the steps and walked out until he reached the same bench that he and Tina had used on their first day together. Should he try to see her? Or just let things go? How could he explain, when he didn't understand anything himself? She was furious with him, otherwise she would not have run off like that. He wasn't certain why, but he accepted the blame. He was not fit company for anyone, not this week, maybe not ever. He hadn't been able to protect her from Ed. Then when the man had been standing there, right in front of him, he had done nothing, nothing at all, except shake his hand. He still couldn't understand that. On top of everything else, he was still waiting to hear from Masback and the committee. Could he take the job? Should he take the job? Would it even be offered? This was supposed to be a week of vacation. Instead, all the unknowns were driving him crazy, like a thousand little demons from hell. One at a time, no sweat, but in an army they were formidable.

TINA DREAMED AGAIN of her father. His face. Tom's face. David and the blond Bathsheba. Ophelia. The laundry room at home, St. Francis, doves, rabbits, pearls, old women in black, and Pandora's Box. Now that she was awake, again, thinking of the bar reminded her that she had never gone by to check on it. Curious. What was real? Memory? Or Dreams? She usually remembered most of her dreams. A lot of people remembered none. She had been surprised to learn this. Over half her friends could not recall their dreams at all. The others could remember bits and pieces, beginnings and ends, but often not in color. This too surprised her because she usually dreamt in full-blown, living Technicolor. Today she would have settled for a dreamless sleep, just a pleasant brief nap, a restorative. She did not normally sleep during the day, only when she was as tired as she had been today, times when she had not been able to get her normal sleep — midterm exams or finals, paper deadlines — times like that. Today she woke up feeling logy, dissatisfied. Nothing in her dreams had really frightened her, yet she was left with a sense of discomfort or disorder. And a headache.

Tina walked into the bathroom and took two aspirin. Coming back through the front room, she stopped by the window to check the sky. It was going to rain. She knew it. Across the street she saw a small, white poodle running along the sidewalk. Cute little dog. Feet going a mile-a-minute. Behind the dog came its mistress, just now passing the tree straight across from Tina's house. An old woman in black. Maybe it was a raincoat? With a hood? It could almost have been a robe and cowl from her angle. As the woman scurried after her pet, Tina got a view of her, first from the side, then from behind. It looked like the same woman from the chapel last night. The one she had thought was Italian. What was an old Italian woman doing here with a French poodle? In her dream, that other woman from the chapel had grown wings and become a dark angel chasing a white rabbit. Rubbing her temples, Tina was sorry she had ever napped.

ON THE WAY BACK from the pier, Tom walked down the main drag. He felt restless, edgy and hungry mostly because his regular, daily routine had been disrupted. Instead of running early, he worked on the portrait. Now he was paying the price by feeling restless, irritable, and discontent.

Judging from the foot traffic, he guessed it was getting close to noon. The whole scene was new to him because he had only driven it before, and that but once when trying to find the address of his rental apartment. Looking around, Tom saw all the usual beach resort businesses: Souvenir shop with postcard racks and coffee cups painted in green with pictures of the pier. Drug store having a sale on toilet paper and Kodak film, packaged in yellow. Jewelry store with one window showing diamonds and emeralds, the other showing plastic beads and cheap watches. Surf shop selling boards with a distinctive blue and white logo, probably a world champion, though he did not recognize the name. Florist on the corner advertizing roses.

Ahead of him, Tom saw a curious sign, almost like a marquee. From a distance, the figure on the sign looked like the nymph on bottles of White Rock mixes. Who was she supposed to be? Echo? A naked nymph from Greek mythology kneeling on a rock above a pool of water, little fairy wings on her back, but they had the story all backwards, Tom thought. It was Narcissus who looked into the pool, not Echo. Closer up, the sign itself was not that detailed. It achieved its effect by copying the exact pose of the nymph on the bottles. Power of suggestion. After all, you can only do so much with glass tubing. Most curious was the neon halo above the nymph's head. It made no sense until he read the name on the darkened-out window: Angel's. Angel's Tavern.

The door opened as a couple walked out, laughing. Young, happy and carefree, the man slapped her on the rear, playfully. She giggled.

"Stop it, Gary," the woman said. Distracted, she did not see Tom and bumped into him, just enough for him to feel her breast on his forearm. "Oh, I'm sorry," she said, looking up at him. "Hey, Good-Lookin', you're kind of cute."

"And you're kind of drunk," her partner said, firmly taking her arm and leading her down the street. Tom watched them go, still feeling the softness of the woman's touch.

"Excuse me, buddy," a man said, stepping around him to go into the bar.

"My fault, sorry," Tom responded, moving back a pace.

Through the open door, he could see half of a pool table, the balls scattered on the green felt surface. Over the table hung the standard-issue, bar-room pool light. On the wall beyond the table was a lighted sign for Budweiser beer: red, white and blue. To the right of the sign, a barmaid was just delivering a tray of drinks to a group sitting at a small, round table. She was wearing a low cut, skimpy outfit, trimmed with yellow lace, showing plenty of leg because the skirt was little more than a frilly brown tutu. The jukebox was blaring out the latest somebody-done-somebody-wrong type of song, sad and so very slow, tugging at your heartstrings. Tom absorbed all these details in the brief time it took for the door to swing open and swing closed.

The scene staggered him like a blow to the back of his knees. He had never wanted a drink so badly in all his life. He could taste it. He could smell it. A wave of desire engulfed him. Even with the door closed, he could still hear the music calling to him, like Greek sirens high on a cliff: "Come to me. Have a drink. Bourbon and water. My baby left me. Take me. I'm yours for the asking."

Tom knew these were crazy thoughts even as he thought them, but he could not stop their coming. His legs actually shook as he stood there, in front of the bar. If he chose, he could reach the door handle without moving. He could be inside where it was warm and friendly in a matter of seconds. Wine, women, song, salvation — all for the price of a drink.

With that thought he felt a sudden flush of relief. He had no money, thank God. He could not get a drink even if he wanted. His wallet was back in the apartment. But just as quickly, his mind leaped in the other direction. He did have money — a single one-dollar-bill, folded over into a tight little square, kept in the pocket of his running shorts. Money for emergencies. Phone calls. He could get one well-drink for that dollar. One drink was all he needed, just the one.

"Well, hello. I dare say if it isn't our distinguished candidate."

Tom heard the words from behind him. He turned to find the professor of Victorian literature from the university. Tom didn't say a thing but just stood there looking at the man in surprise.

"Has the Angel got your tongue?" the professor asked, laughing. "But don't mind me, dear boy. Merely my attempt at humor. I see you have discovered our local watering place. Little early in the day for me, but I am meeting a colleague for lunch."

What colleague could he be meeting here? In a place called Angel's? In the middle of The Shore? Tom tried to remember the man's name, but could not, even though he did remember reading one of his articles.

"Looks like I'm a trifle early. Shall we walk a ways?"

Tom fell in step with the older man, not even questioning or noting the direction they took.

"If you haven't tried it yet, I fully recommend this next establishment. One of the better eateries in the area."

Tom looked into the window of a small Italian restaurant they were passing, just a few doors down from the bar. It had red-checked table cloths, with a sign on the window reading: "Now Serving Breakfast, Lunch and Dinner."

As they walked, Tom and the professor began to talk, mostly the older man at first, with Tom gradually joining in, more and more, the farther they walked. History of the university. Cultural activities available in the area. Local community theater. Life and literature. Tom asked about the article he remembered reading. The professor confessed that it must be something quite old because he hadn't published in years. Early on he did well enough, but then he just seemed to run dry. Sad but true. Tom wondered how much the drinking had to do with it, but he didn't ask. This morning the professor didn't look the least shaky, and Tom could smell nothing on his breath. Could he have been wrong about the man? At the end of the second block, the professor stopped and looked at his watch.

"Well, I should be heading back. My friend may be there by now." Almost as an afterthought, he turned back to Tom, saying, "You're welcome to join us, if you like. My treat." The look on his face was indecipherable.

"No, thanks," Tom said, finding that the words came easily now, suddenly natural.

With a nod, the older man turned around and headed back toward Angel's. Tom could see the sign blinking on and off in the distance, but it no longer held any allure. Why had the professor led him two full-blocks away from the bar, he wondered, only to offer him a drink, now? Tom watched the man as he walked away, a small figure in a tweed coat and a Tyrolean felt hat with a feather in the brim. In the summer? The professor reached the next corner and crossed against the light. Tom watched for another minute, then turned for home, still trying to remember the man's name.

ON SHEER WHIM, Tina decided to call her best friend, Grace, in Paris. Whim or was it instinct? she wondered. Tina did not even know what time it was there. What was the time difference? USA to France? Tina was dialing the number before she had decided whether or not she should. This was going to cost a fortune! As the connection was being made, Tina thought about her friend. What a great name for a girl in Catholic school, but Grace had hated it, growing up, because the nuns seemed to expect more out of her, just from having the name.

"Grace, is that you?"

"Tina Marie! My God, it sounds like you're in the next room. This is great. I was just thinking of you!"

Only Grace called her that. It went all the way back to fourth grade in Sister Chastity's class. The sister insisted that Tina's name must really be Christina Marie, for Jesus and Mary. Her parents had to vouch for her before the sister would allow her to be called Tina in class. Only Grace still called her Tina Marie. Just hearing her say the name cut through all the years of their friendship and now through all the miles that separated them.

"It's not too late?"

"No. Not at all. I was just about to go out. Night club, no less. Tres chic! What're you doing? What's happening in California?"

They talked in shorthand, finishing each other's thoughts. All the old friends, the news. Believe it or not, Grace could see Notre Dame from her apartment window. Is that too much? On and on they talked, until Tina finally got around to what was really on her mind.

"Hey, I met a guy."

"Oh, yeah? So tell me!"

She did. Everything, from start to finish. All the doubts, confusion, the ripped blouse, Tom's gentleness. The portrait. The tide pools. The kisses. Running out of the restaurant. The chapel last night. On and on, until she could think of nothing else to say.

"What do you think?"

"Do you really want to know?" Grace asked.

"Yes, sure I do."

"Okay. Listen up, Tina Marie. Grab this guy. Got it?"

"How can you say that? So quickly?"

Grace told her. "I've known you for twelve years. You're my very best friend, so here goes: Every boyfriend you've had in all that time you dumped when he got too close. Every single one of them. Two weeks, three months — it doesn't matter — too much pressure and out the door. This guy is for real. I've never heard you talk about a man this way. I can hear it in your voice. You wouldn't have called me if he wasn't the right one for you. I can see it from here. Remember now, Notre Dame is right outside my window. Do you hear me? From Our Lady straight to you. I can see it all the way through this skinny little telephone line. From five thousand miles away, I can see it. Grab him and don't let go!"

AFTER LEAVING THE PROFESSOR, Tom headed for his apartment. By the time he got there, he had made up his mind. He was no longer shaky. In fact he was very clear-headed and in total control. He would pack his bags and get out of this town. My God, he had almost slipped. If he could come that close to drinking again, then this whole idea had been a mistake. One bad mistake.

Tom glanced at the portrait of Tina. The pad was still open, propped up on the chair, where he had left it earlier. He had done a good job. It captured her youth and innocence. She was the best part of the whole week. Tom still didn't understand what had happened the night before, but he knew there was no future in the relationship. He should have known better in the first place. A clean break was the best thing for both of them. Closing the artist's pad, he carried it into the next room, so he didn't have to be reminded of her. Had he used her as a distraction? Something to wile away the hours until he heard from the committee? If so, he owed her an apology.

The telephone rang. It was Dr. Masback. In spite of his resolution, Tom felt his pulse rate begin to rise.

"Congratulations, Tom. The committee conferred by phone this morning. You're our choice, a unanimous vote of outstanding. Can you come in Monday and sign the contracts?" he asked, but went right on talking without waiting for an answer. Tom knew the professor assumed he would say yes.

Damn it! Tom silently cursed. Why me? Why now?

Masback continued talking, "I'll make some more textbook suggestions and help you get enrolled in your own classes, but that should be no problem. We're a small department. There's always room for one more in the seminars."

Tom had expected the call, of course, some kind of a call anyway. Now that it had happened, he forced himself to feel nothing. A small dry sadness, perhaps. Certainly not the elation he had expected. Nothing like the scenarios he had played out in his mind during the last couple of days.

Even while Masback continued talking, the Tom of today saw the Tom of yesterday as he would have received the news.

Outstanding, you say? That's great. What a boost! He had done it. Yes. Goals fulfilled. Accomplishments. Nothing was impossible. The real Tom of today laughed, knowing this was all an illusion, a fool's errand. Trailing after the joy came the self-doubts. The university would see right through him. He didn't have the full qualifications. My God, the Kent State shootings were just four months old. This was no time to be teaching college. Did he actually think he could make a difference? Yes or no? He could, one minute. He couldn't, the next. Off and on for two full days, the fantasy Tom had done this. Yes he could, no he couldn't. Round and round. As the professor continued talking, the real Tom only half listened, caught up in his own thoughts.

"You might want to think about using the text that was ordered for that class because they've already come into the bookstore, but it's up to you. Do whatever you like —"

Just yesterday Tom had imagined how this very call would affect him. How happy it would make him. But that had been the fantasy Tom. Now the call merely left him flat. Sure, he had done it, but so what? He could feel no satisfaction from what Masback was telling him. He dared not. Nothing was ever that simple, especially not for Tom. Suppose he gave in to this emotion, this happiness, and let himself dream. What then? Side-by-side with the satisfaction would come the terror. Ice cold terror coursing through his body. Self-doubt and fear.

It was not worth it. It was far better to feel nothing. Standing to the side, the real Tom watched his own reaction. How could he be like this? Was he schizophrenic? Ever since he could remember, he had experienced this duality of emotion. Even as a child, pride and self-loathing came together and fought, integral parts of himself. He had struggled all his life to control those conflicting impulses. In Vietnam, he had succeeded. Feeling nothing, he had achieved so much control that it almost killed him.

For a year now, in recovery, he had been learning to feel again. Was this where it got him? Would he never, ever, just be normal? Masback was winding down, ending the call. What was he saying?

"I'll be in my office all Monday afternoon. Just stop by and see me. I'll arrange for parking, again, but after registration, you'll be able to park in the faculty lot, permanently. A nice perk, don't you think? Tom?"

"Yes," he responded, "a nice perk."

"Congratulations again, Tom. We're very happy to have you on board. You should be pleased with yourself. Have a nice weekend. I've got to run. Goodby."

TINA KNEW SHE HAD an umbrella somewhere, but it would take too long to find it. Instead, she just threw on a wind-breaker and a floppy hat, before setting out for his apartment. She had made up her mind. Grace was right. Whatever was going to happen, she would have to be the catalyst. She had too many feelings, too many unanswered questions. Walking with a determined stride, Tina pushed on, moving through the very emotions she usually tried to avoid: confrontation, challenge, and fear. Grace was right. Her best friend really did know her.

Maybe she had been right last year, too. Grace had asked Tina if she were choosing elementary education because she was afraid of the adult world. Suddenly Tina saw herself, forty years from now, a retired spinster schoolteacher, loved and adored by thousands of seven-year-olds. Grace hadn't even meant to hurt her. It was an idle comment, made in general, as they talked about careers. Maybe she was right. Teaching could be a career, but it could not be her whole life. She didn't want to spend her life alone. She had to stop running from every relationship. Somehow, she had to explain everything to Tom, before he left town, never to return. She had to take a chance.

All her life, it had been: play it safe, don't rock the boat, keep your head covered, stay out of the rain, think before you leap — how many more of them were there? Platitudes? Plans for living? Philosophies for the cowardly? She climbed the steps to the second story, never slowing her pace, opened the door and walked in, all a single motion. Tom was standing by the dinette table, putting a shirt into a suitcase. The physical reality of the suitcase stopped her cold.

"What are you doing?" she asked.

"Packing."

Simple, direct, straight to the point, but she could be just as direct. "You turned down the job, didn't you?" No answer. Tom just stood there with a folded shirt in his hand. "Are you coming back?" No answer again. "What about us?" Still no answer. Oh, God, it was too late. She had lost him. Tina could not stand this silence, this voiceless dismissal and rejection. "Can I at least have my portrait?" she blurted out. It was hers by right. Hadn't he done it for her? "Where is it?" she asked.

"In the other room," he said, then quickly added, "but I can't give it to you. I'm sorry, but I have to take it with me."

He actually looks surprised, she thought, almost panicked by her request, her demand, as if he had never even thought of giving it to her because he didn't want to lose it.

Who had he done the portrait for, if not her? Take it where? A thousand miles from here? Or one hundred? Wherever he lived. What was he going to do with it? Keep it on the wall like some memorial to lost love? Suddenly, she understood. A memorial. Yes, it would never be a talisman, a token, a work of art, or a thing of magic, it would be exactly that — a memorial. He would hang it on a wall, in memory of what might have been. "Maude Muller" was the name of a poem she had memorized in junior high. "Of all sad words of tongue or pen, the saddest are these — it might have been." He was going to leave, go back to wherever he lived up north. He was rejecting the university's offer. He was rejecting the chance to fulfill his dreams, all the wonderful things he had told her. He was rejecting her. Afraid she was going to be sick, she turned and walked out the door.

NEVER MOVING from the suitcase, Tom watched the top of her head disappear down the steps. He wanted to go after her, but what would he say? She was still furious, and he had no idea why. Today it was just one more element in the stew, one more reason he could blame himself. He fought off the impulse to follow Tina by using the same technique he had been using to pack: Don't
think. Keep busy. Just go through the motions. He placed two neatly rolled pairs of socks next to his folded shirt,

followed by the clean underwear. Only two shirts and a pair of pants still remained on hangers, but, instead of finishing, he walked past the closet and into the kitchen where he poured a glass of water. He was suddenly parched.

What are you feeling, Tom? Dr. Dick used to ask him at the VA hospital. The psychiatrist had a chart of cartoon faces up on the wall, each of the faces labeled with an emotion. Angry. Lonely. Sad. Happy. On and on. Like Snow White's dwarfs, except there were dozens of them, not just the seven. During one of their sessions, when Tom was struggling to talk about Vietnam, the doctor pointed to the chart.

"Show me what you're feeling, Tom," he said.

The first time Dr. Sallivant asked him, Tom couldn't believe he was serious. "Show you a feeling on a cartoon chart? Are you kidding me?" It was the silliest damn thing he had ever heard, but the exercise lost its humor when Tom couldn't do it. He could not go from his insides to a cartoon character's outsides. "Son of a bitch," he remembered saying, over and over, as he stood there in front of the poster, feeling like a child.

During the weeks he was in the hospital, Tom learned to match the words with the faces. Happy is the smiling face. Mad is the frowning face. Sad is the crying face. But that was as far as he could go. He could match the words to the physical characteristics on the poster, but he could not match what was going on inside himself to either the words or the pictures. Inside himself, he felt pressure, nothing more, just pressure that he must control. That was the best term he could find. Atmospheric pressure, he could understand. The swelling of a balloon, he could see. Tom could relate those phenomena to himself except for one important difference — he had control over what he felt. He could not control the atmosphere. A balloon could not control its own expansion. But Tom could control what he felt. He could put the lid on the pressure. Control it. Use it. Make it work for him. In combat he was cool, icy cool. No panic. No hesitation. Look. Compute. React.

Tom knew the imagery now, but he didn't know it then. Dr. Dick asked him if his mother had a pressure cooker? Tom did not remember until the doctor described the little whistling, rattling gadget on the top. No, his mother didn't own one, but his grandmother had. Yes, yes. That was exactly what he did, what he could do. Keep his emotions under control. Inside. Safe. When he needed to release some steam, so to speak, he'd get drunk. Or he'd go to the firing range and shoot off round after round until the pressure eased off.

"What happens inside the pressure cooker, Tom?" the psychiatrist asked.

"What do you mean?"

"What happens to anything inside the cooker?"

"It gets cooked."

"Yes. Just like you. The insides don't get any stronger, Tom. They break down, they get cooked. Softened. If there's enough water inside the cooker, what do you get?"

He did not know, so he shrugged.

"You get soup, Tom. Soup."

Tom supposed it was a partly valid analogy, but like all analogies, it couldn't be applied logically or consistently. Good grief, soup and cooked meat? Perhaps it was just a scare tactic that the psychiatrist was trying to use on him? He even asked the doctor if that was the point of the analogy.

"Are you trying to frighten me? Is that what this is all about?"

Instead of answering him, Sallivant asked another question, first placing his hands together, under his chin, as if he were praying or getting ready for the Here's the Church, and Here's the Steeple routine. Tom thought the pose was a psychiatric affectation. Something he had learned in medical school, perhaps in Psychiatry 101.

"What happens if you run out of water, Tom? In the cooker?"

"You run out of steam, I suppose."

"What happens if the little gadget on the top is screwed in?"

Tom didn't know what he meant because he'd never seen his grandmother's cooker close up. He followed the doctor's logic. If the gadget released the steam but was screwed in tight —

"You go off like a fucking hand grenade, Tom!" the doctor shouted, interrupting Tom's thoughts.

Dr. Sallivant moved his elbows to the desk in front of him, cupping his hands into a ball.

"Boom!" He reenacted an explosion by throwing his hands apart, up into the air. Here's the church, watch it blow. "Just like a fucking hand grenade. You. Bits and pieces of you, everywhere."

He should never have phrased it that way. Logically, Tom understood the doctor's analogy, but when the clearing in Nam flashed through his mind, he shut down. Once again, he saw his friend, Bruce. Tom felt himself go totally flat, void of response. Control it. Don't feel. Don't think. He and the doctor spent the rest of the hour looking at each other, hardly speaking. Tom never told the psychiatrist about the clearing.

Back in present time, Tom could feel his heart pounding in response to the memories. Sweet Jesus! He felt himself losing control. He'd been doing just fine until Tina walked in. Everything was safely in hand, but seeing her that way, so suddenly, almost broke his resolve and threatened to push him to the breaking point. Now Tom understood what the inside of that pressure cooker would contain: The desire to drink, a phone call from Professor Masback, the pain in Tina's eyes, the tempting offer of the fellowship laid out on a silver platter, perhaps the same kind of platter Salome used for the head of John the Baptist. But that thought made him think of Bruce. Enough of this! Tom thought, as he slammed the water glass to the counter. A man could only take so much. It was time for him to leave, on a dead run, if necessary. He saw the blood before he felt the pain. The glass had shattered, cutting his hand. For a long time, he stood there, looking at the blood, then slowly he began to cry.

THE STORM BROKE just as Tina reached her own porch. The first clap of thunder seemed to come from some great distance away. Must've missed the lightning, she thought. But the next flash she did see, off to the west. Several seconds later, the thunder followed, announcing a freak summer lightning storm. The rain came then, but she was barely touched by the first few drops. In minutes it was pouring, but she was safe inside, cozy and secure. Alone with her thoughts, she curled up on the couch and cried for a while, but the tears soon passed, sooner than she might have expected. She thought of what Grace had said but dismissed her friend's advice. What did she know? After all, Tina had broken up with people before. It always hurt for a little while, but then you got on with life. No big deal.

Tina decided this breakup hurt less because she had just met Tom a week ago, not even that long, really. Thank God she hadn't let herself fall for the guy, or it would be worse. There was something to be said for keeping your walls up. You stayed safe and secure. Feeling nothing, she went into the kitchen, made a sandwich, cleaned up, and then sat down by the front-room window to watch the storm. She took one bite but then put the sandwich down. She was not really hungry. No appetite. No feelings. Just she and the storm, on the other side of the window.

TINA HAD NEVER TURNED ON the inside lights, so she could see him clearly as he walked up to the porch, carrying something in his hands, covered by a plastic coat. Numbly, she waited for a knock, but none came. What was he doing? She leaned forward in time to see Tom prop a package against the porch wall. He looked above him, then moved the package to a different place. Out of the rain, she guessed. It finally dawned on her. The portrait was in that package. Tom was giving it to her, after all. He stood up, glanced at the door, hesitated, but then turned to leave. He was just going to walk away, without a word, without a goodby. Tina barely knew his last name, so how would she ever find him? How could she even send him a thank you note? No, she thought, this was not right, not right at all. Before she knew it, she had gotten up and was at the door, pulling it open.

Softly she called his name, "Tom."

He turned, as if he weren't sure he'd really heard her voice, until he saw her standing in the darkened doorway. "I'm sorry," he said. "I didn't think you were home. The lights aren't on."

If they had been on, would she have seen him? Or would he have sneaked the package onto the porch and slunk off into the night? Was that a little melodramatic, or was that the truth? "Come in, please," she said.

He hesitated, then bent down to pick up the package. "It's your portrait," he said, handing it to her.

"I know." When she took the package, she saw the bandage wrapped around Tom's hand. "What happened?" she asked.

"I cut myself."

"You'd better sit down and let me look at it," she said. "You're still bleeding."

"It's all right," he said.

"Shut up and sit down. I bandaged up enough little boys this summer to be an expert."

SHE CAME BACK with a box of bandages, tape, gauze, some disinfectant, and a towel for his wet hair. The towel was maroon, just like the one she had with her that first day on the beach, the towel that hit him in the stomach. *Did she remember?* he wondered. While she opened up the box of bandages, Tom dried his head as best he could, one-handed. He gave the towel back to her.

"Thanks," he said, "I needed that."

"Sure," she answered, folding the towel and putting it on the floor. "Okay, let me see the wound."

"It's not really that bad," he said, as he unwrapped the handkerchief from around his left hand.

"It still needs to be disinfected."

The instant she touched his hand, all his resolve started to melt away. His toughness evaporated. How could he ever think of leaving this woman? What had he been thinking?

While Tina worked on his injury, Tom took a deep breath and summoned up all his will power. This would not be easy, but it had to be done. She must never know what her gentle touch was doing to him. It might have been so different, under different circumstances.

"There," she said. "Is that better?"

"Yes, thanks."

She did one final inspection and then left to return the bottle of peroxide and the bandages to the bathroom. Yes, he thought, it was better this way, meeting face-to-face, rather than sneaking off without a word. He would explain to her, make her understand. She returned and sat next to him on the couch. He just sat looking at his hand, wondering how to begin.

At some level, Tom still wished it could have been a clean break, clean and pain-free, but it was wrong to leave things unsaid. Maybe they could stay friends, at least? What could he say?

"Well, what happens now?" Tina asked.

"Right to the point," he responded, smiling. He was the English major, the word-merchant, and yet she was the one who broke the ice.

"I guess so," she answered. Tina paused for a minute while Tom was searching for words, but when he still did not start, she continued. "I'm sorry for running out last night, Tom. When I saw you and Ed at the bar, everything got so complicated, I just had to get out of there."

"Did you want me to hit him?" he asked. "Is that why you left, because I didn't do it?"

"Oh, no. Is that what you thought?"

"Yes," Tom said. He nodded and shrugged. "When I found out that you were gone, I thought it was because I had let you down, failed to defend you —" Tom felt sheepish, but he was also confused. If she didn't want him to hit Ed, then why had she run out of the restaurant? "Why did you —?" he started to ask, but she held up her hand to stop the question.

"Let me try. I've done a lot of thinking about it," she said. "First, I hate physical violence. It terrifies me. I really was afraid you were going to hit Ed. I didn't want you to, but I was afraid you would."

"Yes, but I didn't, so why —?" he started to ask.

"Why did I run?" she said, finishing the question for him. "Yes, I know that doesn't explain everything." She paused, took a deep breath, and then continued, "When I was a child, my home was violent, and not just my father, my mother, too. You'd never know it today, to meet my mother, she's so sweet and quiet, now, but it was no picnic back then."

Tom was used to hearing such horror stories in AA, but he never suspected that Tina came from such a background. "So, you were upset and had to escape — is that it?" he asked.

"That's part of it," she said, "but not all. After my parents' divorce, my mother went on a rampage and eventually had a nervous breakdown. I was sent to live with my cousins until she got out of the hospital. Violence terrifies me, but it also means abandonment."

"I don't understand," he said. "I didn't abandon you —"

"I saw the phone number in your trash," she said quietly.

"Phone number? Oh, you mean Maggie's?" he asked, remembering how the number got there in the first place. "She wrote it on some paper towels in the market."

"And —?" she said, staring at him.

"And what?" he asked, totally confused until it suddenly dawned on him what she must have thought. "Tina, you didn't think Maggie and I — that we had —?"

"Yes," she said. "What else was I supposed to think?"

"She did give me the number, Tina, and she offered more, but I never took her up on it. Honestly. Please believe me —"

Tina did believe him. He looked too sincere to be lying, and it would be just like Maggie to go after someone else's — she was about to think "boyfriend," but she stopped herself. "I do believe you, Tom. I'm sorry," she said.

"I understand, now," he said. "You were right to suspect her, though. She's not much of a friend."

"That much I figured out, but thanks for telling me the truth, Tom. It helps. I really thought you'd slept with her."

"— and abandoned you," he said.

"Yes."

"I didn't — I wouldn't do something like that."

"I see that now," she said. "I'm sorry, Tom. Really sorry."

"It wasn't your fault, Tina. Any of it."

"But it was, partly," she said. "I let everything else get in the way, too.
This is my senior year. That's important all by itself, but I also have my student teaching ahead of me, too. I've been nervous and edgy over that, almost worried sick, to tell the truth. I'm sorry."

"Don't apologize," he said. "I can relate. All the interviews and meetings at the university were driving me crazy — but Tina, don't worry about the teaching. You'll do fine. I can tell."

"There's more, Tom."

Uh oh, he thought, watching her. Just the way she said it looked bad. "What do you mean?" he asked.

"There are times when you just disappear, even if you're sitting in the same room with me."

"Disappear?" he asked, a little confused.

"Like with the portrait. You just tune me out, as if I weren't there. I don't think you even know you do it, but it makes me feel — well, just like with the anger — abandoned — like when I was a child."

"I see," he said, looking back into his own past. He had heard the same thing before, but in a different context. So many years ago. "When I was in high school," he started out, "a girl once told me I turned my personality on and off like a spigot, like a water tap. I've never forgotten what she said — Vivian was her name. She may have been trying to tell me the same thing, I think."

"Maybe so," she said, cocking her head quizzically, as if reading something in his expression. "What happened to her?" she asked.

Why, Tom wondered, *did Tina have to ask that?* "She died," he said. "It was the year after we graduated, in childbirth. Nobody dies in childbirth, not these days, but Vivian did. Guess that's why I thought she stayed with me, her memory, I mean. She was the first of our class to die."

"I'm sorry," Tina said. "I had no idea."

"How could you?" he responded.

"Was she a girlfriend," Tina asked.

"Sort of. We dated for a little while, but I didn't have time for a relationship, not with living and breathing sports the way I did. Guess that I must've hurt her, too, just the way I did you. I'm sorry, Tina."

"Oh, Tom," she went on, "I didn't mean to dredge up any old, painful memories."

"No, it's okay. It really is okay." And it was. Tina had helped answer something that had always bothered him. Now he finally understood what Vivian had meant. He did not like it, but he understood.

"Would you like something to eat?" Tina asked, hesitantly.

"Maybe in a minute or so. I've got to tell you something, first." Should he just go for it? he wondered. Why not? She had been honest with him. Tom took a deep breath. "I'm an alcoholic, Tina. A sober one, now, for almost a year, but still an alcoholic." Good Lord, it was so simple, so very simple once the words were out, but what a relief it was. He felt so much better by finally being honest with her. "It's probably the most important thing you need to know about me, but I couldn't tell you before this."

Tina did not look shocked by the revelation, but she did seem a little surprised. She explained, "I'm sorry, but when I hear the word alcoholic, I think of old men in trench coats, drinking wine out of paper bags. You don't come close to that picture."

"Thanks for that much, anyway," he answered, laughing.

"No, I didn't mean that —" she started to say.

"It's okay, Tina, really. It's okay. I still think the same way, a lot of the time."

"So, that's why you didn't order a drink last night," she said. "I totally misinterpreted everything, then. I thought you were refusing to celebrate with me. Oh, that's almost funny," she said, laughing to herself.

"I should've explained long before last night," Tom went on. "I haven't had a drink for almost a year now, but the idea is still new. I couldn't tell you before because it's still hard to say the word out loud. Alcoholic," he practiced saying it, as if testing the waters. "I'm not comfortable using the term outside of AA meetings yet, and sometimes not even there."

It felt so good to be honest with her. As he talked, Tom wondered why he could not have told her before? She was not running away now, in spite of hearing his deep, dark secret. Maybe it was something more? Did he choose not to tell her just so he could be normal, if only for a week? Whatever normal meant? To live some kind of deluded fantasy? Tom realized how foolish such thinking sounded when the reality of his life was being alcoholic and learning how not to take a drink. Without sobriety, he had nothing.

AS TOM TALKED, Tina began to understand. Not just about him, but about her father. If Tom was an alcoholic, then her own father was an alcoholic, too. She had considered the idea before but never set it into context, never said it aloud, and never asked her mother, but he had to be an alcoholic. Everything Tom said fit her father, too, all the behaviors, the broken promises, and the pain. It didn't excuse the things her father had done, but at least she could understand a little more, a little better. Tina listened to Tom and thought about her own family. It was all the same thing. Tom called it a disease. She didn't know if she could buy that completely, in broad theory, but in the specifics, she could. Her father was sick. She had no problem believing that.

While Tom was talking about a drinking bout in college, she remembered an incident from way back in her own childhood. She was having a slumber party at her house. It was late, but all the girls were still awake, talking and giggling on the floor of the living room. The front door opened and in walked her father, obviously drunk, staggering drunk. Her parents were already separated by then, but her father still had a key to the house. "Just in case," her mother had said. *What could she have been thinking?* Tina wondered to herself, now.

"What's going on here?" her father had muttered, stumbling into the room.

Tina remembered being so mortified and scared that she was frozen there, under a blanket. All she could do was watch.

"What a cute little girl," he said to Grace, who was sitting on an ottoman. "Come here and give us a kiss."

"I wouldn't kiss you for a million dollars," Grace said to him. "You're disgusting."

How could she talk to him, like that? Tina listened, amazed that her friend would say those things to her father.

"Play hard to get, will ya?" her father said.

"You're drunk," Grace responded.

By this time, Tina's mother had come into the room, attracted by the noise.

"David," she shouted at him, "Stop it. Look what you're doing. These are little girls."

Her parents argued for a while, until her father left. Tina's mother locked the door after him. *Why then?* Tina wondered. *After he was gone?* She remembered the room's being very quiet as her mother told them all to go to sleep. No more fooling around. It was too late.

"Was that your daddy?" one of the girls whispered.

Yes, that was her daddy. What might've happened, she wondered, given slightly different circumstances? What might've happened? Tina shuddered, thinking about it. She and Grace talked about the incident the next day. When Tina defended her father, saying that he really hadn't been drinking, Grace just looked at her.

"He was drunk, Tina. Just like my Uncle Bill."

"No, he was all right."

"Tina, he was drunk. I know. People shouldn't be like that. He may be your father, but he was stinking drunk."

Grace broke through Tina's denial, simply by being honest with her. Over the years, she continued doing it, pointing things out when they were wrong or when Tina was trying to color them differently. She was a true friend, one to be grateful for, one to treasure.

Thank you, Grace, Tina thought, turning her attention back to Tom who continued to talk, on and on, out of an obvious need to tell her everything, to unburden himself. They stopped to make some sandwiches, then went back later and made two more, each of them surprisingly hungry. They even finished the sandwich Tina had made earlier. Still later on, they moved from the couch to the kitchen, as she made some popcorn, moving the popper carefully back and forth over the flame. Tom continued to talk as they went back to the front room where they could watch the storm. Talk and more talk. The thunder and lightning passed, but the rain was ongoing, pleasant, soothing. Finally, Tom seemed to wind down, relaxing a little.

"Good grief," he said, suddenly. "My sponsor will kill me." He laughed.

"What do you mean?" she asked, reaching for more popcorn.

"I think I just did my inventory."

"What's that?"

He explained the steps of the AA program. You wrote something called an inventory of all the good and all the bad things about you. A personal inventory, he called it. Tom explained the rest of the steps, what they were, how they worked, speaking almost with a sense of awe and reverence. Listening, she understood why. Anyone willing to do all the things he spoke of would be changed in the process. Doing the steps, he called it. The inventory reminded Tina of confession in the Church. She was also aware of how many times God was mentioned in the steps Tom talked about.

"Are you religious?" she asked.

"Not at all. Just the opposite, really. I was raised in a very orthodox Protestant church, but I quit going when I was eighteen, after a minister accused me of being a heretic." Laughing, he said, "I probably was a heretic. Someday I guess I'll have to make amends to that church and to that minister." As Tina listened, Tom explained, "AA is a spiritual program, but not religious. I learned that from an old man named Singing Sam."

Did everyone in AA have nicknames? she wondered. He had talked about Big John, Betty G., and Contractor Dave. It must have something to do with being anonymous. What was Tom's nickname?

"No one tells you what you have to believe," he went on. "The individual finds a personal Higher Power, or a personal God, one that really works for him — or her," he added the last phrase after looking her way. Tom continued, "I haven't even named my Higher Power. Sometimes it's just the power of the group. Twenty people in a circle, all staying sober together."

As Tina listened, she thought of Christ's disciple, Doubting Thomas. He had trouble believing, too, at first. She thought about her own faith, comparing what Tom was saying to what she believed. She had gone to other churches with her friends and been to several weddings and funerals in other denominations. Only within her own church did she feel the presence of God, completely. She liked the ritual. The genuflecting and crossing. The kneeling. The bells and incense. Church never failed to touch her soul.

Listening to Tom, she was happy for what he had found, but equally happy for what she had. Sometimes she took her faith for granted. It was good to be reminded. She especially liked some of the testimonials by priests who claimed to have been touched by God. Tina understood because it happened to her, too. Maybe not a physical touch but something spiritual, psychic. She believed in God's guidance.

"Didn't you mention being in the service?" she asked, curious as to why he'd said nothing at all about that part of his life.

"Yes," he responded, softly, after a pause.

Tom did not continue, but remained silent for a long time after that. Tina looked at him once or twice, wondering if he had fallen asleep, but he was just staring out the window. She was content with the silence. The silence and the purifying rain.

MY GOD, HE THOUGHT, *I was going to skip right over Vietnam, just as if it had never happened.* Is that what he wanted, just to blank it out? Maybe so, maybe so. He had told Tina about everything else — growing up, high school, college, even some stuff after coming home — but not one word about the service. Should he tell her? Did he have a right to do that to her? Did he have a choice? He had come this far. Could he stop now, even if he wanted? God help me, he prayed, with no idea to whom or to what he was praying.

He began by telling her about Bruce. Everything. Things he never wanted to say. All the things he had tried to hide. All the things he had tried to deny. They had gone into the back country as advisors to the South Vietnamese. Their status non-existent. Their function classified. Mostly they trained others to kill. Sometimes they did the killing. Whole villages. Men, even women and children, all armed. Cong. Obvious Cong strongholds. In the field, they were always on the move, one step ahead of death. The tension was horrible. Drugs helped, plenty of drugs, and all the alcohol you could carry and drink. The worst part was getting used to the killing. No matter what you did, scream, cry or throw up, you eventually got used to it. Just one more body in the mud. One more dead Cong in a rice paddy. You counted them like cord wood. Every month new recruits came into the unit, to replace those that got carried out. Some were American, some South Vietnamese. The first rule was never to get close to anyone. Not anyone. Never let your guard down.

They walked right into the ambush. The village elder had sold them out. A friendly, smiling old man. They ran like hell. Blazing away at anything that moved. Bullocks. Chickens. Kids. Women. Old men. Run and shoot. It did not matter. The order of the day was to survive. On the other side of the river, they met up and established a temporary camp. Took a head count. Everyone accounted for except Bruce, his friend with the flaming hair. Three others had fallen, dead on the spot. Eight had made it across the river. No one had seen the other lieutenant fall. Where had he been? Second to the point. Scouting ahead. That night they could hear the screaming. Over and over, until it got monotonous. Horrible but regular. Like fingernails on the blackboard. On and on. Three men had to hold Tom down, to keep him from going back across the river. He had been wounded in the shoulder, and the medic loaded him up with dope, but it didn't help. Didn't even knock him out. They couldn't give him enough to do that, in case they had to take off, again, on the run. They all knew it was the other lieutenant, Bruce. He didn't stop screaming until just before dawn.

Tom could still hear the screaming in his dreams. Sometimes he woke himself with his own screaming in response. Two days later, they went back across the river. They found Bruce in a clearing. His head was severed. His genitals cut off and placed in his mouth. The rest of him was bits and pieces scattered all through the clearing. Ashes from the fire in which they had burned his flesh. They returned to the village and killed everyone they found. The villagers ran, pointing to the north, telling them the Cong went that way, back to the mountains. They killed them anyway. Who could tell? Maybe they were all Cong. There was no way to know. It was easiest to kill them all, just to be safe. Tom lost count. He continued to shoot even after the others quit. Finally, his sergeant stopped him by pushing his gun barrel toward the ground.

"It's over, lieutenant," he said. "It's all over."

After that it was easy. Killing became a simple, pure act. It wasn't even vengeance anymore, just mechanics. Kill them before they kill you. Booze helped. Only one American in their unit did not take the drugs or drink alcohol when it was offered. He joined the unit after they lost Bruce, after they all got hardened and had gelled into a smooth, silent, dope-smoking, violent killing-machine. The new man sat around, reading the bible and praying. He survived three missions. He would shoot at the obvious enemy, but no one knew if he would shoot a suspected enemy, so they watched him, scientifically, superstitiously. The men started saying that he was going to get them killed with all that bible-reading. You couldn't trust a man who wouldn't get high. One day he disappeared in the field. Two shots. They took cover, backing off. All Tom could remember about the new man was his home town, Cincinnati, Ohio, the home of Procter and Gamble. Ivory Soap was 99 and 44/100's percent pure, but there was nothing pure in Vietnam. Tom was certain one of the other men had killed the new guy, before he could get them killed.

The following month, the unit was commended. They would never get medals because, technically, they did not exist, but the colonel quietly praised what they had done. By the end of the tour, only Tom and one other man survived to come home. The other man, a sergeant, was discharged the week after they returned from his last fire fight. It was the only reason he made it back. The unit was in a supposedly safe perimeter camp. No action for miles. They all got loaded that night, especially the corporal they called Crazy Louie, an Italian from Detroit. They always thought of him as a corporal, even though he had usually just been busted back to private. He couldn't go on R-and-R without getting into trouble, usually something serious because he was a born killer. In the field he was the acting corporal no matter what his actual rank. Experienced. Fearless. Crazy. One of the few who really liked to kill. He admitted it, bragged about it. When the Cong hit the camp in a surprise attack, Louie was flying high, ripped to the teeth. Everyone hit the dirt, except for Louie. He took off into the Cong fire, straight into it, dodging, firing and cursing all the way. The unit took off after him, trying to save his ass. The next thing they knew, it was a rout. The Cong fled, leaving their mortar behind. Louie got a picture of himself, grinning, as he sat on the body of a dead Cong. For that he did get a medal.

TINA DID NOT TRY to stop him. She cried a little in places, but she just let him talk, on and on, getting it all out. Some of it was horrible, some macabre, some even funny in a terrible, surrealistic way. She did not laugh. Once she got up and brought them each a Coke to drink. Tom continued to talk even while she walked into the kitchen. He was still talking when she got back. She tried not to move in case it might distract him, but she knew he would not have noticed, most likely, no matter what she did. Finally he started to slow down. Perhaps it was human nature? He saved the worst for last. She didn't think it was the worst, but he seemed to think so, and that was all that mattered.

BY THE END OF THE YEAR, they were famous. The luckiest unit in the sector. His men trusted him, implicitly, without question or hesitation. In the last six months, he had lost only one man, and that had been the man's own fault. Knifed in an alley outside a whorehouse. Stupid. In combat, not a man fell for six full months. Wounded, yes, sometimes, but they didn't even worry about a couple of bullet holes. They all came back alive, over and over, no matter what the assignment. Tom seemed to have a sixth sense about ambushes. If he didn't spot one coming, one of the South Vietnamese guides did. They worked together like a machine, a finely tuned and oiled killing-machine. If he had pointed them into the barrel of a howitzer, they would have gone, without question. He was lucky. They all said it. He tried to stop the talk, but it was useless. They believed he would bring them back. When the unit took R-and-R, the roles were reversed. Tom stayed drunk and loaded for as long and as hard as he could. They always carried him back to the base and put him to bed.

One morning, they were rousted out early and given a hush-hush assignment. Tom was so drunk, the men had to half-carry him onto the chopper. He threw up in transit. When they were put down in the middle of a small field, he was still so shaky the sergeant had to read their orders and find their position on the map. Once the chopper was out of sight, the medic gave him a shot of something to bring him up. It worked. They had the greatest drugs in the world. He was suddenly wide awake and alert, super-alert, to the point of being hyper, nerves frayed, but at least he could read the orders. They set off, following the map. After an hour, the sergeant called Tom up to the point because he couldn't tell which trail to take. Just as Tom knelt down by the sergeant's side, they were hit from behind. Tom looked at the trails, made a snap judgment, sending the men down the trail to the right while he provided cover fire. One, two, three. All ten of them ran up the trail, as he sprayed the jungle behind them. Just as he turned to follow the men, he was lifted into the air by a tremendous concussion. Four hours later, he was found there, ten feet off the trail, half-deaf, but still alive and without a scratch on him, just knocked silly. The rest of the squad were dead. He had guessed wrong, and they all died.

"But you can't blame yourself for that!" Tina spoke out vehemently, breaking in as if she must, watching his face the whole time.

"It was my decision," he said, turning away from her to look out the window. "My decision sent every one of them down that trail."

After two weeks in the hospital, his hearing came back, the eardrums still intact, and he was reassigned to another unit. His reputation preceded him. Instead of being lucky, now he was a jinx. They all believed it. Even he believed it. He started getting loaded in the field and stayed that way. On a mission, the sergeants were in charge. He gave an order only when he absolutely had to, and then he was so damn careful, so afraid of making another mistake, that even the corporals started acting on their own initiative, instead of looking to him. They seldom returned from a mission intact. Their losses weren't heavy, but they were steady. One or two died every time out. Who was going to be the next? they all wanted to know. Tom was so drunk one night in a fire camp that he slept right where he sat. Sometime during the night, he was awakened by a hand shaking his shoulder.

"Sir, wake up, sir." He never knew who delivered the message, but he understood it. "Watch your back, sir. The men are talking."

It had come to that. His own men were going to get rid of their jinx. The next day he scanned the unit, trying to determine who it would be. It was more difficult with this group because he had been so screwed up, for so long, that he did not really know them. Finally, Tom decided it had to be a shifty-eyed private from Atlanta. He seemed to do nothing but complain, all day long. Still hungover and shaky, Tom walked up to the man, handed him his own side arm, and turned his back.

"Go ahead, do it now!" he told the private.

The other men watched with interest. A couple mumbled something, but no one moved, no one interfered. Tom turned around and faced the private, holding his own arms straight out from his sides, offering himself as a target, a sacrifice. The man just sat there, looking stupid, the gun hanging loose in his hand.

"Well? Are you going to do it or not?" Tom shouted at the man. Finally, he reached down, took the weapon back, holstered it, then turned and walked away. Tom soon had a new reputation. Instead of being a jinx, he was a nut case. "Looney! Absolutely friggen crazy!" was what they said. But he started giving orders again, and the men started following them. And they all started coming back from the missions.

"I can't tell you how badly I wanted him to shoot me," Tom said, looking at Tina, wanting her to understand. "At that point, I was ready to die. I wanted to die. I just didn't want to take anyone else with me."

Word got around quickly. He gained a new level of respect from some of the men, those who thought he had been bluffing and had pulled off a magnificent con, with bravado. He gained new respect from another group, too, those who knew that he no longer gave a shit, just like them. Little by little, they started working together, grudgingly, slowly. In time they became a cohesive unit. They still got ripped when they were in reserve or on leave, but not so bad in the field. He became a good leader again. He no longer had the reputation of being a jinx or lucky. Now he was careful and good. In their last six months, they survived together, all but two. He still remembered those faces and the letters he had written their families. Tom stayed mostly sober and did his duty. Before he knew it, his eighteen-month hitch was up. The colonel called him in and tried to get him to sign on for another tour, blowing the usual patriotic smoke. When Tom did not respond, the colonel walked right up to his face and looked in his eyes. Tom did not flinch. Finally, the colonel just sighed and dismissed him, saying only, "Good luck, son," as Tom backed out of the office. His men gave him a goodby party and that was it. The war was over for Tom, finally over.

He was in Saigon, awaiting his outgoing orders. He partied like everyone else, but mostly the drinking was in control. After all, he was on his way home. It was over for him. One night in a Saigon bar, a captain from his division sat down next to him. They made small talk. The captain wished him good luck, stateside.

"Sorry to hear about your unit," he said.

"What do you mean?" Tom asked.

"You don't know?" the captain asked. "They all went down, two days ago, every friggen one of them. They drew some OCS shavetail virgin shitass for a lieutenant, and he led them right into a crossfire. Sorry, Tom. I should have just kept my mouth shut. I thought you knew."

Tom stayed drunk for a week. It was all his fault. If he had been there, they would still be alive. At the end of the week, they poured him onto the plane for home. He was drunk for the whole flight. Drunk when he hit the stateside base. Drunk when he went to the discharge ceremony. All he had to do was sign the papers. Instead he passed out in the chair while waiting. He came to in the detox unit of a VA hospital. They cleaned him up, dried him out, and started the counseling. He was discharged as a civilian, clean and sober. For a while, he did all right. Got a job in aerospace, settled into a new life. Then the dreams began. Nightly for a while. The VA shrinks could not help him. He started to drink again, mostly so he could get to sleep at night.

Little by little, the drinking got worse, until his boss called him in for a talk. He was a Korean War veteran and covered for Tom.

"Tom, I don't mean to interfere in your private affairs, but when it affects your job performance, I don't have a choice."

"I've had trouble sleeping lately," Tom said, trying to stem the confrontation early.

"I've been there, Tom," his boss responded. "I know what it's like. It's more than being tired. You've got to knock off the drinking."

Tom didn't even try to deny the problem. He just nodded and promised to do better. Out of loyalty and gratitude, he kept the drinking down to a bare minimum. He knew it affected his performance, so he stopped drinking at lunch, and he came in every day, hangover or not. He was getting by. The company already had a piece of the lunar contract, but Tom was not assigned there. When the boss transferred him, thinking a change would do him good, Tom's attitude changed. Here was something he could believe in again. Tom had not been able to believe in anything so strongly since before November of 1963, when JFK was shot. He became a workaholic, hardly drinking at all, and even started an MA program at the local college. He got great recommendations, a promotion, and partial credit for the success of the project. Neil Armstrong's speech was the high point of his career with the company. The next day he went on a three-day bender and would have been fired except for his boss.

"This is the last time!" he was warned. Tom was totally baffled. He had just gone out to celebrate.

Within two months, he was called into the boss's office, again, and given a choice: either go through treatment or be fired. He chose the treatment. It was the best thing that could have happened to him. He was lucky to be alive. From there Tom went on to talk about the past year, since getting out of the hospital. The English course he had taken from Dr. Masback. The staying sober. All the events leading up to his being considered for the fellowship. How he had almost taken a drink that morning. The dreams. Everything. He even went back and talked about the father he barely knew. His mother's dying when he was in high school. Everything.

WHEN HE FINISHED, they just lay there on the floor, holding hands. His breathing deepened, and he was asleep, lightly, easily. Exhausted. Tina cried a little more while she watched him sleeping, until she too drifted off. She never knew how long they slept because she had no idea when they started. They woke almost together, both ravenous again. After eating all the crackers and cheese she had on hand, they raided the refrigerator and devoured everything else resembling food in the icebox. When they finally paused, Tom thanked her for listening. He looked into her eyes for a long moment, but then glanced away as if he were embarrassed, or even more, as if he were shamed.

"You have nothing to be ashamed of, Tom," she said.

"You don't know."

"Yes, I do. I heard it all."

Side-by-side, back on the front-room floor, they watched the storm, lying on their stomachs, listening as the rain picked up in tempo. It felt like the thunder and lightning could start again, at any moment. Tina could sense the electricity in the air. Her pants crackled when they rubbed on the carpet.

"What did you tell the university?" she asked.

"Nothing yet. I'll phone them Monday."

"But you got the job, right?"

"How did you know?" he asked, looking baffled.

"They would be crazy not to hire you."

"I got the offer, yes." Tom said, looking away, but added nothing more. He just rolled over onto his back, staring at the ceiling.

She watched Tom's profile, waiting for him to continue. Why is he still holding back? she wondered. After everything he just said? And what did the suitcase mean? Was he just going home for a couple of days, planning to return when classes started? No, she understood what his silence meant. He was going to turn the university down cold. He had already decided that this afternoon, whether he would admit it or not. But how could he turn them down, now? After tonight? Every judgment, every instinct told her that Tom needed to take the job, to follow the dream. She would have to ask the question because he would not volunteer the information, on his own. Perhaps he hadn't even admitted it to himself.

"Are you going to take the job?"

In one breath, he sighed, saying the words as he exhaled, "I can't." His voice was neutral, dull. "I can't do it."

"Why not? Are you afraid?"

"Sure. I'm terrified. But that's only part of it. Just the beginning."

"Go on, tell me."

Still lying on his back, he put his hands behind his head and stared up at the ceiling. He explained that the offer pleased him. That was why he had come down here — just to see if he could get it. It really was a nice offer. But there was no way he could accept the job. He was in the middle of a project at work, something he could not walk away from. He had responsibilities, obligations. Worst of all, he had learned this past week that he would never be able to write about the things he had told her. Never. It was too painful. Too personal. He had writer's block so bad, it wouldn't budge. Professor Masback had given him exercises to help break through the block. He had tried them all over the past couple of weeks, but it was no use. If he could not write, he would be wasting his time taking the offer, going back to school.

Tina watched him, utterly fascinated. Tom had delivered the entire speech with no inflection in his voice. None at all. Dull and flat. She wondered if he actually believed what he said. She didn't. She knew better.

"If you can talk about it, you can write about it."

He rolled over, in order to face her. "It's not that simple."

"Don't patronize me. You need to write about it. You need to keep on talking about it. Even I can see that. You need to un-bottle it all."

"I just did," he said, continuing to look at her. "With *you*."

"What about me?" she asked.

"What do you mean? You were wonderful. I can't begin to tell you what it means to me, your listening, your understanding. I haven't told all of that stuff to anyone else, not another living soul. I couldn't with the military psychiatrists, and I couldn't with my sponsor, only with you.

I feel freer now than I ever have. But I should never have laid all that on you." He could not look her in the eyes. He had to turn away, rolling onto his back again, where he returned to staring at the ceiling. He was still ashamed. There was something more.

"I mean what about *me*?" she asked again. "What happens now? You turn down the university, go back home to work, and we shake hands? Is that the idea?"

"I can't stay. I would if I could." He rolled over again, facing her on the floor. "Don't you know that?" His hand reached out to touch her hair. She knocked it away.

"Don't do that."

"I'm sorry."

She looked at him, understanding and yet not understanding. Part of it was her. Tom was running away from her, too. This time she rolled onto her back and put her hands behind her head, staring at the ceiling.

"Is it me?" she asked, afraid of the answer.

"No! How could it be you?" he said. "It's me. I'm not ready for anything like this, anything serious."

"When will you be ready?" she asked, never shifting her position or taking her eyes from the ceiling.

"I don't know. I'm way too new at this. We aren't even supposed to get into a relationship during our first year of sobriety."

"I thought you said you had a year?" she asked, turning her head to see his face.

He was slow to answer. "Two weeks from today, but that's only part of it. I couldn't —"

"Yes, you *can*," she said, sitting up and turning to face him. She wrapped her arms around her knees. "I know you better than you know yourself. I can certainly wait for the two weeks. How about it?"

"Are you teasing me?" he asked, looking deeply into her eyes. "I can't tell," he confessed. "But if you're serious, please, please don't be. You just don't understand. It isn't that simple."

Tina watched his face as he spoke, moving into his deadpan routine about how everything was so complicated. How he was an alcoholic. How his company needed him. Not once did he mention how much he wanted to accept the university. How much he loved the idea of teaching there. How much he wanted to write. She had seen all these things in him, this week. Where had all those hopes and dreams gone? How could he just pretend they never existed? Worst yet, he never once mentioned her, how much he liked being here with her. They were good together. Couldn't he see that? He was looking at her, talking to her, but he did not see her. He just said that she did not understand, could not understand. She understood only too well.

"I do understand, Tom. It is just this simple. You are one big chicken shit." She had never talked to anyone like this before, not out loud. "You hear me? Chicken shit."

"Tina, please," he said, looking surprised at her language, almost pleading with her to stop. Tom reached out a hand to touch her arm. She knocked his hand away.

"Don't touch me!"

She got up on her knees, looking down on him from her vantage point. She was feeling really angry. Looking startled, he just stared up at her.

"Let me tell you what you should do," she continued. "No, better yet, let me tell you what you *are going* to do."

She could feel the intensity of her own stare, as if her eyes could ignite a forest from sheer sparks. She shook a finger under his nose as if he were six-years-old.

"Are you listening?"

"Yes."

"First of all, you are not going to leave me. Me. Tina. Sitting right here in front of you. Understand? You will stay here, with me. Second, you are going to take that job at the university. Got it? Third, you are going to be a writer, one damn fine writer. Do you hear me? Say something."

"Yes, of course I hear you, but you really don't understand. It's not that simple."

"It is just that simple," she hissed, making a fist and hitting him on the chest.

Surprised at herself, Tina paused. Had she ever hit someone before? She could not remember, but it felt so good that she did it again.

She continued, "It is exactly that simple, so fucking simple you are the only one who can't figure it out. And they're going to give you a PhD?" she taunted him, this time hitting him on the arm. "What a genius! It is exactly this simple, just like the ABC's." She hit him again, and once more for emphasis, falling into a rhythm. First the chest, then the arm.

"You are not going to run away from me!" When he did not respond, she hit him again. "Say something!" He started to move his mouth, but nothing came out. So she hit him twice more. Pause. "Say something!" Twice more, harder. With each blow, she could feel something being released inside her. Years and years' worth of fear, tension and anger.

TOM WAS TOO SURPRISED to know what to do. She wasn't really hurting him. The blows were almost mechanical, as if she were working out on a punching bag. A ritual act. Jesus, what was he supposed to say? He sat up and tried to restrain her, but she started hitting him faster and harder. When he tried to catch her hands, it seemed to trigger something even deeper in her response. Now, she was all over him, like a fury, hitting as hard as she could. Crying and striking out with both fists. Hitting his chest, his arms, his face, his stomach.

"You are not going to leave me!" she shouted, over and over.

All Tom could do was grab her and try to ride it out. He got both arms around her, but she continued to punch him, using short little jabs. When he tried to pin her forearms, she butted him with her head.

"Genius!" she sneered. "Stupid, stupid, stupid!" She hit him anywhere her fists could reach. "Damn you! Damn, damn, damn!" Her blows increased as if she were just getting warmed up. "You will not leave me. I hate you. I hate you." She smashed him with a fury.

"Please, Tina, stop it," he said, trying to control her. "Don't do this. I love you!"

She stopped so suddenly, it surprised him. He lost his balance and fell back onto the floor, halfway dragging her down with him. She pulled herself loose, getting up to her knees again, above him. She was almost out of breath, gasping for air, with her hands still clenched in front of her. She stared at him. Face expressionless. Her eyes boring into his. Breathing deeply.

"Don't ever say that to me unless you mean it! Not ever!"

He said it again. "I love you, Tina."

"You better mean it," she said slowly, working for air. Never breaking their eyelock, she leaned down and kissed him. Deeply, passionately, eyes wide open, sharing her erratic breath with him.

"You will take that job," she said, gradually beginning to breathe easier, more steadily. She kissed him again, lighter this time, almost a peck on his lips. Then she kissed him once more, longer and deeper. "You will stay here, with me, and you will be a writer." Still looking into his eyes, she crawled up, on top of him, until their bodies fully touched. "Do you understand?"

He could only nod.

Outside, the thunder and lightning began again, in flashes that seemed to light up the whole sky. Booming, roaring peals of sound rocked through the air like waves. Sheets of water drenched the ground and overflowed into the street, becoming a river moving to the sea.

Chapter Seven: Sunday

SHE WAKES, FEELING ALARMED, not certain why until a moment passes. Her bed. Her room. The difference is the hand on her hip. His hand. Something different. A new experience. She is not used to sleeping with someone. Slight, momentary sense of panic until the confusion resolves itself, as her consciousness lifts through the mental fog. Knowledge and memory. Very dark, middle of the night. Some light coming into the room from the curtained window. White light. Street lights. His breathing behind her. His hand on her hip. The whole universe centers on his hand and her hip. Man, woman, birth, death, infinity. Words from the introduction to the *Ben Casey* show, the sequence ending with a cross and the sideways figure eight standing for infinity. All women through all time. She slides back against him, and he moves his hand and arm all the way around her, pulling her close, in his sleep. An embrace. Yes. Exciting, but warm and pleasant, too. It feels so good, experiencing, remembering. Safe, warm, protected. It is raining again. Yes. The rain had wakened her. Not a heavy rain, this time, but just enough to hear against the roof and see against the glass of the window facing the street light. A gentle summer rain. In a few days, everything would be fresh and green.

THE ROOM IS LIGHTER NOW. Early dawn, so she must have gone back to sleep. His hand is gone, so is his breathing. She listens for a long time, then slowly turns her head. But he is not in the bed. He must have gotten up. Is he gone? Listening, she hears his steps in the living room. Turning back, she smiles and settles into the covers, snuggling into the pillow. In the far corner she can just make out her portrait, propped up on the chair, where she put it the night before. Pulling the sheet up to her chin, she smells him and herself, the residue of their love. The muscles of her groin spasm slightly as she gently rubs her thighs together. She had no idea making love could be so good. Who could have known? Pleased with herself. How could she have known? So very good. A crazy memory comes to her from years ago, when she was in elementary school. Walking home in her uniform, the neighborhood kids teasing her, chanting: "Tiny Tina from Saint Augustina." Over and over, until she cried. The past was the past. Finally. Who would have thought? Who would have known?

SHE MUST HAVE DOZED again. Slowly, she stretches, letting the covers slide off her neck and shoulders. Moving her head to gaze at the portrait, she snuggles back down. The light has shifted with the coming dawn, so that now the silver pastel of the crucifix is particularly real, almost a living glow coming from the dark corner. Staring at the cross, she again thinks of her grandmother. The unbroken generations of women in her family, reaching back through time. Unknown faces. Unknown dreams. Not quite awake, but out of habit, she starts her morning prayers. Prayers of grace and thanksgiving, petitions, sliding into the familiar confessional, Father forgive me for I have — but she cannot finish as scattered memories of the night before flood back. Father forgive me. Father forgive me for — for what? Forgive me for I have — I have — but she cannot say the word. Her breath quickens. Guilt? But no. Not guilt. Love. Not that other word, either. Not sin. I have been loved. I have. I am. I am. Simple as that. A prayer. Peaceful and pure. Or beyond prayer itself. Worship of the Creator. Hail Mary, full of grace. But that will not do either. Not now. Not in this moment. Love. The cross seems to twinkle. Her pastel face comes to life as the room continues to lighten. It is beautiful. She is beautiful. I am beautiful. Lying very still, she watches herself emerging from the dark. Gently, warmly, her mind remembers the night before, basking in the pleasure. Thoughts are not thoughts but sensations. Feelings joined to pictures. Bodies. Breathing. Warmth. Touching. Stroking. Kissing. Blending. Merging. A moment's pain, soon forgotten. His eyes are blue. The hair on his chest is curly. Strong. Silent. Eager. Patient. How could any of this be wrong? So right. Meant to be. Ordained. Touching. Holding. Kisses on eyelids, cheeks, and temples. Sacred places. Holy places. She feels herself growing warm. Damp. She feels the heart beating in her chest. Stronger. Faster. The tempo rises to match the rhythm of the typing from the other room. She listens, almost hypnotized by the steadiness of the sounds. He is typing. Her portable machine. But he is writing. Tap-Tap-Tap. Clickety clack. Bell of the carriage return. Ding. Tap-Tap-Tap. Listening. Listening.

SHE MUST HAVE DOZED OFF, again, because the room is even lighter, now. Coming up to awareness, she still hears the sounds of the typewriter. Tap-Tap-Tapping. Ding. Did the carriage bell waken her, like a gentle alarm? Tap-Tap.

The muffled sounds are pleasant. Regular. Reassuring. She imagines line after line filled with letters, stretching off to the horizon, like rows of corn. Still lying on her side, facing the portrait, she pulls the sheet up to her chin, moving her knees toward her stomach, curling into a ball. She folds her arms across her chest. Hugging herself. Hugging her breasts. Warm. Pleasant. Secure. Tingling. Her breathing is deep and regular, but, conscious now of her body moving against her arms, her breathing deepens even further, pressure increasing. Each breath is an embrace. She moves her thighs. Flexing. Breathing. Warm. Wet. Miraculous. Immobile, she luxuriates in the sensations. Memories. Hugging. Kissing. Holding. Listening for the typing, she slowly realizes that it has stopped. How long ago? She listens. Nothing. How many minutes pass? How long has she been listening? Then it dawns on her. Full force. The silence speaks to her. He had just been typing. Using her machine. Writing. He could not yesterday. But he did just now. She knew he could. Like the little train. She thought he could. Choo-Choo. Tap-Tap. Tap-Tap-Tap. Afterwards he could. He did. After her. After they. Only after. She soars, a priestess at a new altar, and smiles. Sanctified. Life itself is a prayer. Thank you, God. Hugging herself closer. Happy. Success. Pleasure. Warmth. Exhilaration. Power. Slowly the typing begins again. Tap-Tap-Tapping. Then it stops. His voice, angry. Silence. She holds her breath, willing him to begin again. Tap-Tap. Tap-Tap-Tap. Slowly at first, then faster, moving back into the previous rhythm. She exhales, smiling. Her mind drifts to the future. Next week, her student teaching. Fulfilling. All the children. A warm and pleasant thought. Confident. Ready. She listens.

THE DREAM WAS ABOUT her favorite kitten as a child. Futon. She had named him after a piece of Japanese furniture in her Aunt Peggy's house. He was golden with a pushed-in face. Cute when you got used to him. Such a good cat. Not a malicious bone in his small body. He liked nothing more than to lie in the sun or to curl up in your lap. She feels good and warm remembering. Her mind shifts to the other room. No more typing. Was that a sound in the hall? Lying still, she listens and hears a click, behind her. She holds her breath as the doorknob turns. The bottom of the door slides across the carpet. But not all the way. Teasing. Sibilant. Part way open. He is watching her. She can feel it. Slowly, quietly, she exhales. Breathing in, she smells fresh coffee. Toast. Feels the beating of her heart. His eyes on her. Watching. Holding still, she looks to the portrait, imagining herself in his eyes. She looking at herself. He looking at her. Without thinking, she begins to stretch. Slowly. Straightening her legs, letting the muscles stretch, all the way to the tips of her toes. Wonderful. Instinctive. Rested and Restored. Opening her arms. Releasing her breasts. Reaching out. Stretching. Reaching out to embrace the world.

Epilogue

THEY WERE MARRIED the following summer, just after Tina's graduation. Grace was Tina's maid of honor, and Wayne stood up for Tom. Wayne insisted that Tom get a local sponsor, saying he would always be his first sponsor, but that he needed someone close by. Tom chose Radical Russ, attorney and counselor. They began to talk, slowly at first, but then as Russ opened up to Tom about Korea, Tom began opening up to him about Vietnam. Russ was one of the ushers at the wedding. After much soul-searching, Tina asked her father to give her away. David came alone, having enough sense to leave the latest girlfriend in Arizona. He drank, but Tina never saw him do anything that would embarrass her, his daughter. Tom and David could not get along together, at all, from their very first meeting. They declared a truce of silence, and Tina was just as glad her father lived in another state. Tina's mother, Pearl, cried a lot and said she was very proud of her daughter. Tina was hired to teach in the local school district, in the same school where she had done her student teaching, close enough that she could walk to work.

Tom accepted the university's offer and began his doctoral program while teaching in the English department. He settled into the local AA meetings and stayed happily and productively sober. He still liked to run on the beach, early in the morning. Two weeks after they first met, Tina went to a meeting with Tom and gave him a cake to celebrate his first year of sobriety, a chocolate cake she had baked herself. Three months after they were married, she gave him another one for two years.

In the evenings, the two of them would often walk out to the end of the pier, where they sat on the same bench as the first day they met, holding hands and talking about the day just ending. Sometimes he would read what he had written that day. Together they would watch the glory of God's sunset, the colors seeming to surround them, often in the full range of the promised rainbow.

In the beginning

GENESIS OF LOVE

This book was set up, written and designed using Corel's WordPerfect with Palatino and Pristina as the two main fonts

Made in the USA
San Bernardino, CA
30 October 2013